LIES
OF
THE SAINTS

LIES OF THE SAINTS

ERIN MCGRAW

CHRONICLE BOOKS
SAN FRANCISCO

Some of these stories originally appeared in magazines,
as follows: "Blue Skies" and "Rich" in The Atlantic Monthly;
"A Suburban Story" in Image under the title "The History of the Miracle";
"Saint Tracy" in Ascent; and "Stars" in The Southern Review.

Library of Congress Cataloging-in-Publication Data:

McGraw, Erin, 1957–
          Lies of the saints / by Erin McGraw.
              p   cm.
          ISBN 0-8118-1315-0
              1. Manners and customs—Fiction.   I. Title.
      PS3563.C3674L5   1996
      813'.54—dc20   95-30082
                        CIP

Printed in the United States of America

Cover design and illustration: Brenda Rae Eno
Book design and typography: Sarah Bolles
Composition: On Line Typography

Distributed in Canada by
Raincoast Books
8680 Cambie Street
Vancouver, B.C. V6P 6M9

10 9 8 7 6 5 4 3 2 1

Chronicle Books
275 Fifth Street
San Francisco, CA 94103

For Andrew

Acknowledgments

I owe thanks to many friends and colleagues who read and commented on these stories: Barbara Bean, Leslee Becker, Leslie Jennings Cooksy Riggin, Bo Caldwell, Samuel R. Delany, Caroline Patterson, Anna McGrail, Robert Nelsen, and Brad Owens. Thanks also to Beth Gylys for her kind and speedy help. And heartfelt gratitude to Gail Hochman and Jay Schaefer.

I would like to thank the Ragdale Foundation, the Ohio Arts Council, and the Taft Foundation at the University of Cincinnati for providing support.

The greatest thanks, beyond words, to my husband, Andrew.

CONTENTS

THE RETURN OF
THE ARGENTINE
TANGO MASTERS

Five minutes before her show went on the air, Gwen DeRitter greeted Don, her producer, who glared at her from the studio door. She'd overslept by an hour and a half, and then found the highway access washed out by the last five days of hammering rain, so she'd had to veer into town the long way, stuck behind all of Elerette County's cautious farmers and nervous senior citizens.

"Glad you could make it," Don said now.

"Wouldn't miss it for the world," Gwen said, mopping her face with the towel he handed her—the dash across the parking lot had left her soaked and thinking bitterly, again, about the twenty dollars' worth of grass seed that had been washed from her front yard. Her husband Leo's nursery, which should have been doing forty percent of the year's business, was as still as a church.

"Dry your hair," Don called as she moved toward the booth. "I don't want you dripping on the console."

To appease him Gwen twisted the towel into a turban while she grabbed a Temptations CD from the oldies shelf in case she needed filler. Unlikely today, though. The county was full of farmwives watching their new tomato plants slowly keel under the rain; Gwen's listeners were remembering and reliving every disappointment of their lives. The day before, a woman had spoken sharply for fifteen full minutes about home permanents: how lousy the instructions were, and how crappy the results. Now Gwen tucked a stray hair into her turban, and at the stroke of ten leaned into the mike.

"This is Gwen DeRitter. What's your mind?" While her cued music played, she quickly flipped through the stack of announcements for the quarter-hour break—an F.O.P. dance, Kiwanis, nothing unusual. When she looked up again, one of the lines was already lit, some listener so crazy with the rain he couldn't even wait through Gwen's usual ten minutes of patter.

"Here we go, somebody's ready to start us off. What's your name, and what's on your mind?"

"My name's Mike. And rain's on my mind." The voice was eager, the sort who liked to come on the air and tell jokes. Gwen had a well-known soft spot for the joke tellers.

"We're all thinking about rain, Mike," she said. "I don't have a lawn left."

"Lawn? I don't have a car left. I touched the brakes and the whole front end shot around. Wound up hitting the corner of the post office."

"Ouch."

"Those folks were testy, I don't mind telling you. And the garage estimates five grand on the car. This is a Ford, Gwen, a used Fiesta. Was it ever worth five grand?"

"I don't think so," Gwen said, frowning at the easy way he used her name. Callers often sounded familiar, but this one pulled hard at her memory, and made her nervous. "I hope you had insurance."

"On a Fiesta? Why bother buying a Fiesta if you have to get insurance? I'd think you'd know that."

The voice slotted into place. Gwen swallowed twice and licked her lips. "Rafe?"

"I wasn't sure you'd talk to me if I gave you my real name." He chuckled thinly.

"Well, folks," Gwen said, "this is quite an event. I've got my ex-husband, Rafe Johnson, here with me on the line. How long has it been, Rafe?"

"Eight years and two states. First Kentucky, then Missouri."

"And you're back here just to visit, right?"

"It's nice to be home. I've missed knowing where all the roads go."

"They go out of town. You told me so yourself."

"They led me back, too. It's good to hear your voice, Gwendo."

"We'll take a break for our sponsors now," Gwen announced, turning off the mike and wiping both wet palms on her turban, rubbing so hard that the towel came unwrapped and her wet hair slapped down against her neck. "What the hell are you *doing?*" she snapped into the speakerphone.

She could hear the shrug. "I had a few things on my mind."

Since Leo didn't listen to the show, Gwen had to recount it all for him over dinner, even though his eyes were vague, his mind hypnotized, she knew, by the thought of a hundred-fifty balled and burlapped dogwoods slowly drowning in his lot. "Rafe went on and on about our crummy little apartment. Every time I tried to cut him off, he'd say, 'They weren't such bad years, were they?'"

"What did you say then?" Leo asked.

"I told him I didn't remember. Calls were stacked up. One girl kept saying it was the most romantic thing she'd ever heard on American radio."

Leo shook his head. "And I missed the whole shooting match."

"We're not done yet." Gwen's voice grew lopsided and hysterical. "Callers wanted to know all about it—where we'd lived, how young we'd been. They kept saying to me, 'Well, we know your secret now,' like it was a big joke. They started telling me about the marriages they'd seen crack up. One guy actually moved his girlfriend in with him and his wife."

"Greedy," Leo commented.

"So stories are gathering steam, the lines are jammed, and I'm thinking that maybe this will be all right. Then some gal says she has a question for Rafe, if he's still listening. She wants to know if hearing my voice brings it all back, the good times and the bad. 'Rafe? Are you out there?' she says. 'You let us know.'" Gwen, who was a good mimic, pinched her voice and troweled on the drawl.

"You didn't have to put him back on the air," Leo said, finally setting down his knife and fork.

"Don was standing right outside the booth. He was still mad at me for getting in late, and he loved what was going on.

He would have called in his own questions if there'd been room on the phone lines."

"So Rafe calls back."

"So Rafe calls back. He asks me if I remember how we went to drive-in movies the first year we were married. 'Uh-huh,' I say. But he wants to *talk* about it, how I brought a jar of peanut butter and a bag of apples. We were the only ones in the lot actually watching the movie because we could go home to a bed. He got a huge kick out of that."

"Cheap date," Leo said.

"Three hours of this. I'd cut in for commercials and announcements, and he kept pulling up memories. He must have built a shrine to that marriage."

"Don't you remember?" Leo asked.

"That's what he kept asking. You could hear all those people out in radio land thinking, What a sweet man. Still carrying a torch. And Don gloating outside the booth."

"That doesn't answer the question. Do you remember?"

"No, honey, I don't." She went to Leo, lightly touched his hair. "It's been a long time. When you're happy, you don't need to sit around remembering."

"Tell Rafe that," Leo said, reaching up to pat her hand.

"I'm trying to work it in."

A person didn't have to do much to become a celebrity in Elerette County; Gwen's picture appeared in the paper from time to time, and she had become used to people pointing at her in parking lots and introducing themselves when she worked the station booth at the fair. "I try never to miss your show," women, especially, told her. "I like to hear what's on people's minds."

"It's PR," she explained to Leo when he pointed out that her admirers made them spend twenty extra minutes at the grocery or hardware store. "If people feel like they know me, then I'm doing a good job." She was always pleased to stop and chat, sometimes even sign her name across a scrap of paper fished out of a purse, while Leo fiddled with a display of canned tuna or wrenches.

But none of these folksy encounters prepared Gwen for the interest Rafe's phone calls brought. A reporter from the Indy *Star* showed up, grinning like a wolf and calling the whole business her on-air love affair. It wasn't a love affair, she contradicted him, angry and sweaty from talking to her ex-husband for three hours. Leo was the one she loved. But none of her protests made it into the story, which featured Rafe insisting, "I have never forgotten her for even a second." Gwen's ratings vaulted twenty points, and national affiliates called Don, suggesting that interest existed beyond Elerette County, Indiana.

At his empty nursery, Leo began to listen to the show out of self-defense, and over dinner he asked questions. Why had Gwen cut off that woman with the twin baby girls? Did she think Rafe was telling the truth about moving to Missouri? He sounded shifty to Leo. At night now Gwen had dreams of being hunted across miles of open territory, so she put off sleep, staying up till two o'clock, listening to the rain and jotting down memories of her first marriage.

The second week, she went on the air armed. When Rafe asked, "Don't you remember, Gwendo? Don't you?" she answered, her voice full of tenderness, "There are things from those days I can never forget. One night I made a spaghetti casserole for dinner, and you flipped your plate onto the table and said, 'I don't eat garbage.'"

"I did, though," he said. "Remember your tomato omelettes?"

"One. You ate one tomato omelette once, and then told me that if I put anything like that in front of you again, you would divorce me," she said. Gwen settled into her chair. She had told Leo that morning: If people were so set on hearing about it, they were going to hear about it all.

"You were no Julia Child," Rafe said. "Those lead cakes!"

"I'm surprised you don't remember these things better. That cake—it was lemon—fell because you slammed the back door so hard the window fell out and broke."

"I remember perfectly. The power went out, we ate pork and beans out of cans by flashlight, and then we danced, since the radio had batteries that worked. I taught you the tango that night."

"Nice try. We took tango classes at the Y."

"The classes came later. We began in our living room. I showed you the *ochos*."

Another call came in, and Gwen gladly put Rafe on hold. "What's on your mind?" she said.

"I tango, too." A man's oddly stern voice. "I came here after the *tangeros* left, and I was furious to have missed them. They're famous in Buenos Aires. They teach all over the world."

"They didn't speak much English," Gwen said. "They'd do these gorgeous steps, and then we'd have to go out and get them coffee because they couldn't order for themselves."

"Listen to me! I called because I have something to tell you," the man said irritably. "They're coming back. Just for one night. They're holding a demonstration class."

"At the Elerette County Y? I'd think famous tango-ers could find a glitzier venue."

"Why shouldn't they come here? People in Elerette County might want to know how to tango. You wanted to know once."

"It was a joke," Gwen said, but the man dropped the receiver before she could explain, and she sighed and turned Rafe back on.

"Okay, I admit it. I knew they were coming back," he said. "I got a flyer. How about it, Gwendo? Want to brush up your *paso doble?*"

"You forget—I have a new partner."

"We can show him how it's done."

"Believe me, Rafe—you haven't got a thing to show him," she said, and watched the console light up with indignant calls.

Leo came home shaking rain from his hair and whistling "Hernando's Hideaway" at Gwen, who snapped her heels on the kitchen floor. If he wanted to make it a joke, she'd play along.

"I couldn't get three steps in a row right," she said. "Even when I closed my eyes all I could see was Hoosiers pretending to slither across a bordello floor."

"Don't shatter my illusions," he said. "I sat there listening to the show thinking of cigarettes and pouty brunettes who look like trouble."

"Get your mind out of the movies, Paco. Overhead lights and fleshy housewives in shorts."

He snorted and started rummaging in the refrigerator. "I would have paid good money to see it."

"The class is free," Gwen said.

"It shouldn't have been; think of the entertainment value. No offense, honey, but I have trouble imagining you with a rose between your teeth."

She smiled tightly. "Look—the tango masters are here for publicity, to drum up interest. Half the town will be there. Think of it as a community event."

He pulled his head out of the refrigerator and shut the door, his hands still empty. "Half the town will be there to get a look at your ex-husband. You'll have to forgive me if I don't share their interest."

"Don grabbed me the second I came out of the booth today; nineteen people called the station when they couldn't get through to the show. He says I can think of the master class as promotional time for the station."

Leo stopped, his back to Gwen. "Did he say how I can think of it?"

Gwen looked at the kitchen floor. "It's my job, Leo. It's cash in hand. What if you lose all those trees? How can we say no?" She hated bullying Leo this way, and hated Don and Rafe and Leo for making her do it. When she heard the floor squeak and looked up, she saw Leo bent over, his body in the shape of a horseshoe. He had been a gymnast in college, and liked to demonstrate his skills from time to time. "What's this?" she asked, trying to keep the annoyance out of her voice.

"Me. Over a barrel."

"Sorry," Gwen said.

Leo bent further, bouncing until his elbows grazed the floor. "Can I ask for one favor? Don't turn me into a media event. I'll go and I'll watch, but I don't want to meet him, and I don't want any microphones in my face."

"Fair enough. You want to bring something to read?"

"Naw," he said, finally straightening up. "While you two talk I'll learn to tango."

The gym at the Y was stuffed, a sea of clamor; Gwen guessed that two hundred people had shown up. More were still arriving, dropping their umbrellas and slickers in heaps at the doors, adding to the overheated room's thick smell of sweat and wet vinyl. All over the basketball court knots of dancers stood, some embarrassed, some clowning, most of them wearing running shorts and sneakers. The dancers waved to their hooting friends in the bleachers.

Nervousness kept a grin clamped across Gwen's mouth. As far as she could tell, Rafe hadn't arrived yet, but two camera crews had, and there was Don making a jaunty circle with his thumb and forefinger while he hurried around with the soundman. Gwen hid behind Leo, who was rolling his shoulders, loosening up. "Look at this place. A cast of thousands," he said.

"And no sign of the star," she said, scanning the rows for Rafe. On the radio that morning he said he'd be wearing a purple shirt, and now it seemed to Gwen that half the men in the gym were wearing purple. They were pointing at her and waving, and she felt her grin stretch further. She didn't know which she dreaded more: her public reunion with Rafe or the assembled audience watching her stumble through the old, forgotten tango moves.

At the gym's far end, under the scoreboard, stood the four tango masters, who didn't seem impressed by the crowd. They talked to one another, and Gwen wondered whether they had learned more than ten words of English yet. She envied how elegantly they had aged; although their hair shimmered with new silver, they were still slender, and their movements were elastic and prowling. At a signal Gwen couldn't see they took their places, not saying a word.

The volume on the old phonograph was set as high as it would go, making the sound wobble, and the crowd kept hooting and slapping high fives. But even with all the shrieking and banging, once the demonstration dance started, Gwen remembered why she'd wanted to dance the tango. The masters were disciplined and liquid at the same time, haughty, full of pride and sex. One of the men slung his partner away from him so that she skittered across the floor, but when he gathered her back her face was still disdainful, her back furiously erect. Leo moved away from Gwen to a spot where he could see better, and she heard somebody say, "Jeez, they must fuck like rabbits."

She and Rafe hadn't. After an hour and a half of bumbling at the Y, not even able to get the posture right, they'd skimmed away from each other once they got home, embarrassed every time they looked at their paddling feet. But now, watching the masters whip one another around, she was all set to buy into the fantasy again, imagining herself glaring into Leo's eyes until the gym dissolved into a red-wallpapered room where he could rip her dress off.

The music ended on a cracked high note and the tango masters stood for a glassy, uninterested bow. Right behind Gwen a man shouted, "*Bravi! Bravi!*"; she sighed and turned.

"Well, Rafe. Does this bring it all back?"

"Better." He grinned, his hands wide. Under his purple shirt he wore slim black trousers that he still had the figure for. "Memory didn't do them justice."

"This next part's what I remember," Gwen said, nodding toward the masters, who were demonstrating the first slow, sliding step, the set of the shoulders. Behind them the dancers tried to follow, their sneakers squealing on the floor. Cameras whirred and popped. "Again," called the masters.

"This is fantastic!" Rafe said, spreading his hands, stopping just short of touching her. "All these people."

Gwen glanced around to find Leo. He had moved up closer to the masters, and he was frowning, concentrating on the step, which he did better than most of the men. "That's my husband," she said.

"Next step," called the tango masters, pivoting.

"Come on," said Rafe, stepping closer to Gwen and taking her hand. "Let's give them a taste." He nudged his leg between hers and rested his hand on her hip.

"How much longer do I have to tell you no?" she said, pulling back hard and slamming into someone who, when she glanced back to apologize, turned out to be Don, holding a video camera.

"I've just got my volume working right," he said cheerfully. "Now start again."

Gwen looked frantically toward Leo, but he was frowning, trying to work out the pivot with a dumpy redhead.

"You don't need to get his permission," Rafe said, pulling her to him again. This time he held her tighter, forcing her through the steps, shoving her to make her turn, bending her over his arm so fast that her head whipped back. Don shad-

owed them, and when Gwen looked she could see his grin behind the camera.

A space had cleared around them; now Rafe had room to
push her away and snap her back again. Gwen was breathing
hard and trying to move away gracefully, but Rafe kept crush-
ing her against him. She waited until the next breakaway step,
then used her free hand to slap Rafe so hard her own hand
hurt. He caught her before she could slap him again and
wrenched her arm back, pulling her hair with it so that her
head was tilted and her neck exposed. Just then the music
ended, but Rafe made Gwen hold the position for a moment
longer, until the tango masters could come over to them and
nod. "Is the tango," one of them said.

The photo spread in the next morning's *Bugle,* under the head-
line TANGO FEVER, took up half a page and featured a shot of
Gwen dangling over the back of Rafe's arm. In the photo Rafe
had the fabric of her blouse between his teeth.

"I was there," Leo said. "I saw it."

Gwen wadded up the blouse and threw it in the wastepaper
basket. "It was worse than I ever could have thought. And I
thought it would be pretty bad."

"It was something to remember. But the guy can really
tango."

"Jesus, Leo. It would be okay to show a little jealous anger
here. Supportive, you know?"

"You're standing there throwing clothes away. It's not as if
you were mooning around, murmuring his name. Not that I'm
encouraging you."

"You are too rational for my good," Gwen said. Then she

acidly added, watching Leo watching himself in the mirror, "Arch your back more."

At least it was Sunday, so she didn't have to face the station, and could plunge into the chores that three weeks of rain had driven inside: mildew crawling on the windowsills, linoleum around the back door streaked and dim. But once she got to the kitchen, all she did was sit and stare into her murky coffee. She was mooning, she knew it. She was humming. She was remembering the hard weight of Rafe's arm, his growl when he yanked at the collar of her blouse.

He'd known what he was doing, getting her to that Y. Now, looking around her kitchen, Gwen was annoyed at its clean paint, its fussy matched prints on the walls. She rubbed her eyes, furious with Rafe for getting her to yearn, even for a minute, for years that had been such a stupefying failure. She was furious with herself, too, for wishing now she could take a crowbar to the clean walls that held her. At the very least— and this seemed as shameful as any filthy desire—she wanted to dance with Rafe again.

She was still gazing into her untouched coffee when Leo pivoted into the kitchen, his feet inscribing half-moons on the floor. "He didn't dance like that before," Gwen said.

"I didn't think so. You wouldn't have forgotten."

Gwen shuddered. "Did you see the women around him after the class was over?"

"Why are you surprised? He came in like Rudolph Valentino. I'd love to be able to move like that."

"Don't even say it," she said.

He darkened his voice. "I'd come home from work and drag you into my arms."

"I fall into your arms, anyway."

"Maybe once," he said, swiveling toward her and away from her, "I want to force you."

"And suddenly I seem forceable," Gwen said through gritted teeth. "Is that what you're saying here?"

"Lighten up," he said, finally standing still. "I just want to learn the tango."

"The tango masters are gone."

"You're not gone."

"No," she allowed slowly. "But I've forgotten."

"Give it a try. One step will lead to the next."

"No it won't," she said, standing up. "I can't teach you what I don't remember."

"You did it with Rafe."

"He did it with me. Don't ask me to go backwards, Leo."

"Don't ask me to forget what I've seen." He pushed her lightly back into her chair, and she kept her face lowered until he left the room. She didn't want him to see the excited wetness in her eyes.

Don called on Monday morning, while she still had a mouthful of toothpaste. "I want to hurry your famous hiney along," he said. "Big doings down here."

Gwen spat into her hand and said, "Give me a hint, Don." But her dread rose so high and hard she barely listened, even when Don explained about the new markets she would start with today, the station's new 800 number, the interest from as far away as WGN. This was the worst news yet. "Rafe's brought you to the big time, gal," Don said, as if reading her mind.

"Where is he?" she said grimly.

"At home sitting next to his phone, I hope. We've sold a lot of people on his romantic voice."

Shaking, nervous, Gwen drove as jerkily as a teenager to the station, and the engineers looked up when she came in as if they hadn't watched her do her show five days a week for the past eight years. Her first two calls came from local women who wanted to talk to Rafe—they had been at the Y on Saturday night. Had he dated any women since Gwen? Was he ready yet to take another chance on love? "I saw that man dance," said the second caller to Gwen. "I don't mean to hurt your feelings, but they don't come along like that very often."

"No problem," Gwen said. "Rafe, are you out there? Your public wants to know." She was struggling to hang on to her easygoing, cheerful persona, imagining her voice washing out in waves that lapped up against St. Louis and Chicago. But calls trudged in reluctantly, the pauses between them widening. All day she fielded questions for Rafe—women were leaving their home phone numbers, offering favors so astonishingly explicit that Gwen had to keep her hand on the cutoff switch. By Tuesday, when she could feel the pressure of her listeners sitting beside their radios, twitching with annoyance, Gwen started to let impatience creep into her voice. It was just like Rafe, rattlesnake mean, to choose the most public way he could imagine to humiliate her. Did he think she was going to beg? He was out of his mind.

She turned the mike back on and leaned into it. Suddenly, pleasantly, she had plenty to say. "You're back with Gwen DeRitter. You know, we need to talk. We're in an important moment. I think it's just like a certain kind of mean-spirited man to get the women in his life all built up, full of hope and dreams, and then to vamoose. I think this is what we can expect when we deal with the Rafe Johnsons of the world."

Gwen glanced up and found Don across the office. He looked relieved to hear her talking, so she kept goading until the calls began to spill in — the woman whose husband rented a U-Haul during her night shift and moved out every scrap, including her irreplaceable file of family recipes; the mother whose junkie son had been through four rehab programs, breaking into her house and shooting the family dog after one of them; the wife of thirteen years, confined to a wheelchair since an auto accident, whose husband had introduced her to — in order — genital crabs, chlamydia, and herpes. "It wasn't hard to stop believing him," she said. "The second round of penicillin pretty well took care of that. What's hard is having to stop hoping at all."

"You hope and then they shut the door in your face," Gwen agreed. "It's amazing how long it takes us to see that we're getting splinters in our nose."

Gwen had thought that would tip Rafe over the edge; in the end she had been the one to leave him, not the other way around, a fact he was unlikely to have lost track of. But it wasn't until the woman with the plaintive voice of a country singer called and said, "I've got two ex-husbands and I don't care what happens to either one of them, but I'd sure like to have Rafe Johnson teach me to tango," that he finally called again.

"Well, if it isn't Rudolph Valentino," Gwen said.

"It wasn't easy seeing you at the Y and then coming home alone," he said. "I needed a little time."

"Listen, I'm happy to give you time. I'd like to give you even more. But you have a listening audience—a responsibility. Not one of your strengths." Gwen knew she was opening a door for him here; this was his chance to launch into another rhapsody about their life together, how a night didn't pass without his whispering her name. But he surprised her. "I'm better now," he said. "I know my strengths."

"What are they, Rafe? America wants to know."

She could hear from his voice how he was smiling into the phone. "Tango. Classes took a few days to set up, but I've got the Y twice a week. Enrollment will be first come, first served. I've already saved you a place, Gwendo."

"Give it away," she snapped, and cut him off. Later she explained to a furious Don that she'd needed to make room for the callers they'd been waiting for, who finally started to stampede onto every line.

By the end of the week Gwen was calling her show "Rafe Woos the Masses." Don was installing a three-way line so that callers could talk to Gwen and Rafe at the same time, and Gwen could hear her tone grow sharper as Rafe waxed debonair. He talked at length about his need for passion, and Gwen wondered if she was the only one to notice that he'd stopped talking about their marriage. "You've always been a smoothie," she told him, just to let him know she was paying attention, but in fact, she hardly cared, preoccupied as she was with the tension that had begun to hum between her and Leo. She had shown him as much tango as she remembered— a turn, one complicated pass—but he wanted to know more, nagging and tugging at her until one evening she turned around and slapped at his shoulder, missing by inches. In bed that night, Leo bit her like a cat.

The little they talked, they talked about Rafe. Don had explained to Gwen, in terms as formal as a contract, that she would be attending Rafe's classes if she expected to continue her employment, and now Leo wanted to know every word she and Rafe had ever exchanged. So on the night of the first class, Leo drove to the Y while Gwen described, over the squeal of the windshield wipers, Rafe's ability to quote whole passages from *The Misfits*.

Leo snorted. "It's not like he memorized *King Lear*."

"He thought Arthur Miller was an authentic genius."

"Arthur Murray, maybe."

"Cute, Leo." They were still squabbling when they came into the gym, which was crowded but subdued, strangely orderly; people in the bleachers sat as quietly as a concert audience, and the couples on the floor made way when they saw Gwen and Leo. Rafe nodded her over, pointing at a spot in the front of the room. Gwen, feeling as if she were spotlit, jerked her chin at Leo. "My husband."

Rafe smiled. "The lucky man."

Leo smiled back at him—rather, Gwen thought, he bared his teeth. "The new celebrity."

Rafe shrugged. "You make the most of what you've got. I can't believe how long it's taken me to learn that." Then he turned his back and started the class on stretching exercises—shoulder rolls, loose shimmies to isolate the pelvis. Gwen twitched and shrugged through the exercises; the tango masters had never bothered with warm-ups, and for an unbalanced moment Gwen missed her old teachers as she might miss actual friends.

Only after fifteen minutes of stretching did Rafe show the first sequence of long, slinking steps leading to the *sacada,* where the man would push his partner into a tight, angry turn. Rafe went over the combination twice, calling out the counts, and Gwen couldn't hold down her own pride when she saw how quickly Leo fell into the posture. Most of the men behind him looked as ungainly as kangaroos.

"Now the ladies," Rafe said to Gwen, adding over his shoulder to Leo, "Watch. This is what you'll be dancing with." Gwen tilted back her head and smiled darkly, but Rafe held her away from him, at dancing-school remove. He counted *and* one, *and* two, pushing her shoulder when she forgot to move back, and when they got to the *gancho,* the light, flicking kick done with the woman's thigh pressed hard against her partner's, Rafe dropped her hand and said, "You know what comes here."

"I don't even remember how to start," she said. "I haven't tangoed in ten years."

"You and Leo work it out," he said, turning to the record player, gesturing Leo and Gwen together.

Just as Rafe lowered the record player's arm, Gwen cried, "Rafe!" her voice crumbling under all the weight she put on it. Rafe stopped the music, and Gwen heard someone sigh behind her, but she was already beyond embarrassment. "Aren't you here to teach us? None of us knows what we're doing. How are the men going to know when to make their partners turn?" She pushed Leo away from her.

"I'll tell them. That's why I'm here."

"'That's why I'm here,'" Gwen mimicked, letting go of her

last shreds of self-control. "I don't think that's why you're here. I think you're here to make my life hell again."

Rafe led Gwen by the elbow back to Leo, who looked angrily away from her. "Don't think," Rafe said as he restarted the music. "Move when I tell you."

With the music Leo's posture changed; he seemed to grow taller and harder in Gwen's grasp, half familiar, like a dream figure. He stared at the far wall, even though his arm pulled her very close. Rafe, walking in front of the first line of dancers, called out steps and corrections—"Ladies, press your ankles and thighs up against your partners'," he called. "Backs straighter. Leo, hold her tighter." Gwen, who already felt squeezed, began to protest, but Rafe called out, "Turn!" and the words were snapped soundlessly out of her mouth.

On the recovery, as they began the sequence again, Rafe harangued from his corner. "Sharpen! Hold her tighter!" until Leo's arm cut into Gwen's back like an iron bar and he bent her carelessly, too hard.

"Rafe," Gwen finally called back sharply over her shoulder. "Rafe, you're hurting me." But she didn't break away, and Leo whipped her around for another turn.

A
S U B U R B A N
S T O R Y

When the pebble flew out from the gravel truck in front of them and cracked the windshield, Iris wasn't even looking; she had leaned over to tighten her daughter's seat belt. She jerked her head up at the sharp pop and looked into a lattice of hard lines. Lisa, of course, started to cry. "Hush," Iris said, fighting unsuccessfully to keep the snap out of her voice. "It's just an accident." Lisa wailed.

They were on their way to Lisa's third day at school, and the girl had been crying for a week, threading herself around Iris's legs, refusing in the mornings to pull on her own socks. "This happens all the time," the kindergarten teacher had told her, smiling at Iris, but Iris, drained of patience, knew better— she remembered how Lisa's brothers had whooped and torn into the classroom. Now the girl was thrashing under the seat belt as if it were a harness, screaming, "I hate it! I hate it!" Iris pulled over by yanking on the steering wheel, and the car bumped hard against the curb, sending the girl's screams up half an octave.

"You're too old for this," Iris said, trying to still the quiver in her voice. "You're a big girl."

"No!" Lisa squalled, pointing to the explosion of lines. Iris couldn't begin to guess the replacement cost. She sighed, shifted the car into park, and smoothed her daughter's hair. "All right," she said. "Let's calm down now."

"No." Lisa subsided, but Iris could see her calculating a victory; the car had stopped. "It's broken," she said, nodding at the windshield.

"It sure is," Iris said. "But isn't it pretty? Look," she said, running her finger along a line that caught the morning sun in a bright channel.

"Pink," Lisa said, pointing her own wiry finger at another line.

"You wouldn't have seen this if it didn't get broken," Iris said.

"I hate it," Lisa said.

"Me, too. But at least it's pretty." Iris shifted the car back into drive before Lisa could cloud up again, and they made it to school only five minutes late. Lisa dragged morosely into the classroom.

"See?" the teacher said, smiling. "They always come around."

Iris smiled back, too depleted to think of a snappy answer.

She felt tired all the time lately. She had hoped for wide drifts of time now that all three of the children were in school, but her energy dribbled away into PTA and Cub Scouts. If she hadn't known better, she might have thought she was pregnant again; her own body seemed mysterious and alien and exhausting. She stooped for a drink at the water fountain outside

Lisa's classroom door, then went down to the teachers' lounge for a cup of coffee. She might as well stay; she was scheduled for eleven-thirty playground duty.

By the time she made it out to lean against the fence and watch the fourth graders play kickball, Iris's mood was perfectly sour. The preliminary telephone bids for the windshield were each enough to break the bank; Jack would be furious. By the third call she simply hung up and went out to the playground, where she didn't have to talk. The children played ferociously; games ended when some bruised child sat sniffling and shrugging her away, and Iris wondered what her presence there was supposed to do. She had never once prevented an accident.

She listened, keeping a distracted eye on the game, while Frances Holmes fretted about next week's parishwide crab supper. Frances was hoping the door would be at least five hundred dollars. Plans for the outdoor chapel were way behind schedule, but Frances didn't know what people expected her to do without any budget.

Iris sighed and stared unhappily at her feet. Sheer guilt would force Jack and her to go, although seafood made her queasy. Why couldn't the committee have set up a steak dinner? She was about to ask, and nastily, when she heard a child beginning to wail. She looked up in time to see the red kickball catch Tommy Pointer on the throat; the boy dropped as if he'd been shot.

Iris took off. Tommy had fallen hard, straight back, and on the asphalt beneath his head there was a tiny seepage that Iris looked away from the moment she saw it; she could only stand so much.

Tommy was silent, and his face had already turned a rubbery gray. Iris, wincing as sharp pebbles cut into her knees, took his hand. "Tommy? You're all right, aren't you?" A moment passed, and Iris was aware of the boys jostling behind her to catch a glimpse, though none of them made a sound. Then Tommy opened his eyes and pulled his hand away.

"Sure," he said, scooting onto his feet. He wiped his nose with a gritty hand and ran toward the water fountain while his friends jeered. Iris felt a rush of relief, and for a moment she stayed on the ground, too soft with gratitude to stand. When she glanced at the spot where Tommy's head had lain, there was no moisture at all, and she thought it was amazing what a panicky mind could invent.

"They're indestructible," said Frances when Iris rejoined her at the fence. "Did you hear about Pat Kenny's boy?" Iris nodded. Pat's four-year-old, left for a moment in the car, had slipped off the emergency brake; the car had rolled across an embankment and four lanes of traffic before settling underneath a speed limit sign.

"God keeps an eye out," Iris said, surprising herself, and then let Frances go back to costs and logistics. Iris's head pounded with children's laughter and shrieks; she felt like an overfull cup. Five minutes later, when the recess bell sounded and the children formed wavering lines, she had to look away, weak at the thought of looking after so much sweet, unscarred skin.

Iris's sourness lingered and spread to Jack, so that they had spent all weekend sniping at each other. On the drive over, ducking and craning to see through the windshield that he predicted would get them a ticket, Jack said, "We'll get stuck with the Logans. Bill will talk all night about his important work for TRW and his important work on the steering committee and his important work with the Boy Scouts. And then we'll come home and you'll throw up all night."

"We don't have to sit with them. We can't not show up. People expect us." Iris was trying to get the clasp on her necklace to catch, taking deep breaths—her stomach already felt wobbly.

"We certainly wouldn't want to let *people* down," Jack said, pulling into a space by the rectory and jerking up the parking brake. "My head feels like it's breaking in half."

"What do you expect? You diddle around in the basement until it gets so late you don't even have time to take an aspirin. Ben wanted to talk to you, you know. He wanted to show you his project."

"I thought you wanted the water heater fixed. I thought you'd asked me to look at it."

"For God's sake," Iris snapped. "Here. Let me rub your head for a minute. We can't go in there looking like murder."

"Ah hell, nobody notices anyway," he said, settling his head into her lap. She could feel the tightness quivering around his eyes, how hot he was, and she brushed his temples with the tips of her fingers, unable to keep herself from slumping. Her weariness seemed able to deepen infinitely.

"That's better," he said.

"Relax."

"I mean it. It's better." He held her fingers still against his head for a moment, then straightened up.

"It can't be. I hardly touched you."

"Well, it's gone, Magic Fingers. Let's go in. Maybe we can still get home before the news."

But Iris was exhausted; Jack had to help her to the door, where Frances met them and said, "We almost started without you. Thought maybe you'd decided not to come."

"Who, us?" Iris said faintly. "Bells on."

The auditorium seemed to rattle with laughter and the banging of steam tables. Above the racket, Iris heard the buzz of Kay Wendell's wheelchair and winced—Kay had been diagnosed with MS ten years before, only a month after her husband was killed by a hit-and-run driver. She persisted in attending church functions, Iris was convinced, because she could trap people into listening to her pathetic litany. Iris turned, but Kay was already on her.

"Well, you finally made it. I guess I shouldn't expect people with children to be on time."

Iris felt Jack stiffen beside her, and she put her hand on his arm to keep him from bolting. "Nice to see you, Kay."

"How many wee ones are there?" Kay cackled. "Six?"

"Please. Only three. That's plenty."

Kay looked down and fiddled with the controls on her wheelchair. "When you live alone, everyone else's house seems so full of life."

"I see plenty of life in you yet, girl," Jack said, and took Iris by the wrist. "Look, dear. There's Bill Logan. We'll be seeing you, Kay." He steered Iris to a table already heaped with red and white crabs while Iris ducked her eyes and glanced back at Kay, who at least wasn't following them; she had caught Betty and Frank Marsh at the coatrack.

Iris survived the meal by industriously separating meat from shell and then eating the hard French rolls—first her own, then Jack's. Jack and Bill Logan carried the conversation, Jack laughing forcefully at all of Bill's jokes. He wiped his eyes. Iris wished he wouldn't try so hard. By the end of the meal, her plate and lap were covered with crumbs, and she thought of her house and robe with a yearning that bordered on the erotic.

As Jack was encouraging Bill to tell him more about the Scout trip, there was a cry directly behind Iris. She turned to see Meg Price choking and flailing at her husband, who shrank away from her. Meg's shoulders jerked and her face turned the color of iron. Iris scrambled up before she had a chance to think and started pounding Meg on the back, while the woman grabbed her and whined desperately. Iris turned Meg around, clutched her under the ribs, and pulled up so hard she felt something in her own back give. She had no idea what she was doing. Meg was still hacking, so Iris tried it again, half hanging on to the other woman for support. After the third try Meg barked and spat out a piece of shell an inch across that gleamed as it hit the plate. She fell forward, hanging on to the table, and Iris reached for a chair. Her lower back seemed to have separated into distinct, fiery pieces.

The auditorium clamored. People rushed in on Iris and Meg, exclaiming over what they'd seen, congratulating, marveling. Iris's knees quivered, and the damp shadows of nausea swept across her stomach. "Lucky for Meg you knew how to do the Heimlich," Jo Salton was saying. "I keep meaning to learn."

"Instinct, I guess," Iris said. "I just found myself doing it." She saw Jack studying her from across their table, looking startled and uneasy. "If it wasn't me, somebody else would have helped," she said loudly, looking straight at him.

"That's right," Kay called out, whirring over from two tables away. "Anybody would have done as much." Her mouth was bunched up like a paper bag.

"Not that I wasn't glad to help," Iris said.

"Purely human nature," Kay said. "Reflex."

"You know, it's harder than you think. Next time—" Iris began.

"Somebody else will get to do the saving," Kay said, grinning at the speechless Iris until Jack picked up his coat and said that they'd better get back, before someone needed saving at home. He had to let Iris lean on him all the way out to the car; her ankles kept buckling as if she'd been drinking.

Jack stalled a week before he asked, diffidently, how Iris had known what to do for Meg, and Iris looked out the window and told him the truth: "I don't know. I just found myself grabbing her." He didn't ask any more, but she felt him tracking her as she made her way around the house.

She wished he would stop it. He snuck looks from around the newspaper, watched her dry dishes as if she might reach into her pocket at any moment and produce a hissing fuse. "Here," she said, setting a cup of coffee in front of him. "Please just drink this."

"I don't know if I want it that bad."

"What does that mean?"

"You're acting like Joan of Arc at the stake because you fixed a cup of coffee. I didn't even ask for it. What is going on with you?"

"I'm trying to be a good wife. I'm trying to do my job around here."

"Well, quit trying. It didn't used to take you all this effort."

That night, while she was brushing her hair, Jack came and laid his hands on her shoulders with a gesture so proprietary she jerked away despite her best intentions. "I'm *tired*," she said, which was the level truth.

In the morning she apologized, but Jack grunted; mornings were not his best time. And still she felt nervy, full of prickles; she swore at the agave by the door when she stepped too close and snagged her stockings. Late, she drove to the guild meeting snags and all, barely avoiding a dog who got lost in the fractured windshield, and when she was nominated to head the outreach committee, she said with embarrassing passion, "Please! Anybody else." At the break Mary Lou Betts asked compassionately whether everything was all right at home, and Iris smiled, shrugged, and nodded, afraid of what might fly out of her mouth.

At home the kids' noise filled the house, and Iris found she could get by on nods and shrugs, which at least kept her from picking more fights with Jack. He didn't understand; she was scrabbling to keep solid ground under her feet. When Ben came down with the flu, she made Jack take the boy's temperature and dole out antibiotics, afraid of what her hands might do. "I can't afford to be exposed," she murmured as an excuse. "We go to the clinic next week."

In fact, she was in charge of the guild's annual visit to the free clinic downtown, the one committee duty she didn't mind. Iris enjoyed watching the young doctors and nurses who volunteered. The clinic patients were mostly immigrants—entire, enormous families—and Iris listened happily while the doctors prescribed blood-pressure medication and iron supplements for the grandmothers, dark green vegetables for the children. Here was real help; she was glad to be a part of it.

For weeks the women in the guild had been collecting medical supplies from their own family doctors—drug samples, tongue depressors, disposable gloves and basins. The bags of goods always seemed impressive to Iris until she got to the clinic, where the stack of tongue depressors rattled into an empty drawer. A nurse smiled at Iris. "There's never enough," she said.

As always, the women stayed to serve lunch to the doctors and nurses. Iris took on sandwich duty in the makeshift kitchen, where she methodically sliced the ham they had brought and slapped it onto slices of bread. She was good at this; the line of sandwiches was scarcely different from mornings at home.

A woman, one of the patients, slipped into the kitchen with Iris. She was thin and had a lump the size of a tangerine under her jaw. She wasn't supposed to be in the kitchen. The guild couldn't bring enough food for patients, so they tried to be discreet about lunch. Iris wondered whether she should say something or simply escort the woman back out to the waiting area. She stared at the woman's lump; the skin over it was stretched so taut it was lustrous. "Would you like a sandwich?" Iris asked.

"Yes."

Iris handed it to her, watching while she took her first bite. The lump didn't prevent her from swallowing, and so Iris smiled and went back to the ham. "Thank you," the woman said, and then the door clicked softly. Thank *you,* Iris thought, pleased with herself. She made three more sandwiches before she heard the door open again and looked around to see the woman standing with a crowd of children—seven? Ten? The woman looked at her calmly.

Iris felt the small of her back sag. She gestured at her meager provisions—two loaves of white bread, a small ham, and the mustard Renee Cox had remembered to bring. "There isn't enough." She looked at the woman with the lump. "I'm sorry."

The woman said nothing and played with the hair of the boy standing before her, who was looking at Iris with eyes so soulful they seemed impertinent. "Oh, for heaven's sake," Iris said, and began to hand sandwiches around. She would go out to a grocery store. Lunch would just have to be late. The children chewed their dry sandwiches, and she returned to the counter, hacking at the ham. She felt a tug on her skirt. A little boy pointed to the oranges, and she handed him one. "Thank you," he said.

Then Iris heard the door open again, and Renee saying, "What are you *doing?*"

"Things got out of control."

"There are medical professionals out there, volunteering their time for these people."

"Give them these." Iris filled her hands with sandwiches and a few oranges.

"Now everybody wants to eat. Iris, we never feed the patients."

"They never asked before," she said, reaching into the bag for more bread.

Before long, the guild members began coming into the kitchen in shifts to collect sandwiches and oranges. In a minute, Iris told herself, I'll have to go out and get some more. But her hands, greasy with fat, kept slicing and stacking, and she stood at the narrow counter and made sandwiches even after Renee told her that she had made enough, that everyone had eaten. There was still the butt end of the ham, half a bag of oranges. Renee had to take her by the elbow and force her to sit down, when finally Iris felt blind with fatigue. Renee pressed a sandwich into her hand, but Iris couldn't lift it to her mouth.

"We didn't have that much food," Renee was saying. "You know we didn't."

"Hush," Iris said.

Monsignor Laoghrie was calling when Iris walked in her front door, and after him neighbors, half-strangers. People had heard reports that Iris had been bathed in light, had talked in languages no one had ever heard. Suzanne Muller asked if it was true that the oranges tasted like sacramental wine. "Mine didn't," Iris said, talking with her head propped against the wall.

It was after four, and none of the children was home. Iris shivered. She felt naked in the house without their comforting uproar, and tried to remember—she had left Lisa with Frances, but was this the afternoon of Jim's rehearsal? She was hanging up the phone for the seventh time when she finally heard a shuffling at the door. "Hey," Iris called. "There are cookies in here."

Instead of answering, they filed silently back to their rooms, and fear rose in Iris like a quick flood; she set the phone off the hook and went to the boys' room. Jim, facedown on the bed, didn't move, and Ben sat with his back to her, his jaw hard and quivering. Sometimes he looked so much like Jack that Iris caught her breath. "Don't you want anything to eat?"

"No," Ben said.

"What's up? How come you were late home?"

He shrugged. "Leave me alone."

She went to Lisa's room, her mouth dry. Like Jim, Lisa was stretched out on the bed, but Iris heard her sniff and she crouched by the bed, laying her head beside her daughter's on the pillow. "What is it, honey? What happened?"

Lisa edged away from her, and at first Iris thought she wouldn't talk at all. "Sister made us stay. The whole school. She made us all stay after school and said you'd performed a miracle." Her shoulders were rigid. "She said you were holy."

"Oh, honey," Iris said. "Honey. I'm just your mom." She put her hand on Lisa's steely shoulder. "Everything is just the same."

"It is not. Everything's wrecked."

Iris looked at her daughter, who lay with her head twisted away from her. Wildly, she wanted to laugh. "If I'm holy, maybe I'll be a better cook. What do you want for dinner? Do you want spaghetti? I'll make you anything you want."

"Leave me alone."

"You'll see," Iris said. "It will go away in a few days, and you'll see that nothing has changed." She reached out to stroke her hair, but then let her hand drop in the air between them.

Jack came in an hour later, and they looked at each other warily across the width of the living room. "Well," he said. "I hear I'm married to Our Lady of Sandwiches."

"Is that supposed to be a joke?"

"You are some kind of famous," he said, his tone so non-committal that Iris felt like slapping him. "I've been getting phone calls telling me the history of the miracle all afternoon."

"What do they say?"

"It's the loaves and the fishes, right here in River City."

"The food went further than we thought. Nobody thought we had enough, but we did. That's all." She stood blinking at him, her hands clenching and unclenching.

"A committee will be over later to take the measurements for your shrine."

"Listen to me, dammit. I sliced the ham thin, and it went around. Who are you going to believe here?"

"A hundred people say it was a miracle. You say it wasn't. How do I know who to believe? Hell, Iris. How do you know?" He shrugged.

"You never believed in miracles before."

"You never performed any before."

Iris shook her head; frustrated tears were crowding her throat and eyes. "Wait till you hear what Sister Margaret did," she whispered, fighting for control.

"I heard."

"The kids won't speak to me."

"They'll get over it. They're scared."

"So am I. Aren't you?"

"Terrified," Jack said flatly.

That night, after Iris had burned the potatoes and broken two dinner plates while loading the dishwasher, the doorbell rang. It was Sandra, the little girl who lived next door. Her parents didn't belong to the parish, so Iris only saw the girl when she happened to be outside playing, a tiny, weedy thing, smaller than Lisa. "It's late, honey," Iris said. "Do your parents know that you're out so late?"

Sandra nodded. "I hurt my elbow."

"Where?"

"Right here," the girl said, jutting her knobby elbow at Iris, who couldn't see any scratch or bruise. "It hurts," Sandra said. "I hurt it."

"Do you want me to kiss it for you?"

Sandra nodded again, and Iris bent swiftly. When she straightened again, the girl's expression was rapturous. "I knew it would feel better if you kissed it. I'll bet it will never hurt again."

"Kisses don't last that long," Iris said, but Sandra was already backing away, her hand cradling her healed elbow, her face radiant. "Shit," Iris muttered.

"Suffer the little children," said Jack, coming in from the living room.

"Very funny."

"Come on, honey. Kids love saints." He skimmed his fingers lightly up her sides, and she jerked away. "Stop twiddling at me. I am not a saint. I don't do miracle cures."

"Not on the home front, that's for sure."

"Then quit looking at me like you're expecting something."

"Lately I don't expect one thing from you. Some miracles are just too much to hope for."

Iris nearly collided with Ben as she stormed to the bedroom. He was still sniffling, and she rested her hands on his head as they passed. She listened after he went into the bathroom, but he wasn't crying anymore. God*damn* it, she thought.

The next morning the phone was still off the hook and notes were stuck under the welcome mat; Iris had refused to answer the door again after Sandra's visit. Jack left early for work and the kids shuffled and muttered, refusing to look at their mother. When Ruth Dowers, who was driving carpool that week, swung into the driveway, Jim and Ben and Lisa raced out the door like escapees.

Iris trudged into the kitchen. Sugar was scattered across the table and floor, milk was already hardening at the bottom of glasses. The frying pan Jack had used was jammed into the sink, dried egg crusted around its sides. Iris stiffened her arms in front of her. "Shazam," she said. Nothing moved.

There were beds to be made, laundry. But she walked through her house with her hands stuffed deep in the pockets of her robe. She wanted to sit down, but there wasn't one chair in the whole damn house that didn't have ripped upholstery or jabbing springs. She and Jack had said for so long they would get around to buying new chairs. How many nights had she watched him squirming in the recliner by the door, trying to find a smooth space? She felt her heart open to him as if it took a physical fall, even though she had meant to stay angry.

She wandered into their bedroom, vaguely planning to make the bed, but she stopped at the doorway, looking at the one crucifix in the house. It hung next to the window. Iris hated religious art, and had agreed to put up the crucifix only because it had been a wedding present—she couldn't remember now from whom. Someone who didn't know her very well.

She took it off the wall and turned it around in her hand, surprised at its lightness. Cheap construction. Sitting on the bed to relieve her back, supposing she ought to pray, she let her thoughts race away from her. She remembered how, when Jim had been a toddler, he'd sat for hours turning his toy car in tight circles over and over the same patch of floor. It had worried Iris that he'd been so content with the car tracing its own tracks. What had happened to that car? She couldn't remember.

She looked at the crucifix in her hand. The figure of Jesus didn't seem to be in pain. If anything, it looked a little buoyant. She closed her eyes, trying to stop these thoughts, which were probably blasphemous and would bring on swift retribution. She remembered a holy card she had gotten in second grade, showing the Good Shepherd surrounded by dozens of children. His face had been beardless and full of light. Her friend Susan's showed him walking on water, which Iris would have preferred.

"I guess this is your idea of a joke," she said to the crucifix. Two months before she had been closing in on happiness like safe harbor. But now she was right back out in the deep water, and the lights on land were winking out. She got up, hung the crucifix back on the wall and turned away, fighting the habit to touch her lips and murmur "Ad majorem dei gloriam." Old habits, she thought as she left the bedroom.

The local RiteBuy served as the neighborhood town square, and Iris could usually count on running into three neighbors in the cereal section alone. But remarkably, as she hurried through the aisles, she didn't see any familiar faces. Sister must have called the whole town in, she thought. She picked up treats for the kids—cookies that were out of the budget, ice cream. She fingered the oranges, then let them drop back in the bin. She moved past the fish section briskly, but she couldn't help glancing at the glazed eyes of trout, horrible, and beside them neat sets of shad roe.

Jack adored it. On their first anniversary he'd taken her to a restaurant that featured seafood as well as beef; Iris was sure she could stand to look at roe as long as she wasn't expected to eat it. But when the waiter brought their meals, the sight, reddish and coiled like intestines, was too much for her, and she'd spent the rest of the night, first in the restaurant and then back at home, retching.

Now she stepped back when the butcher told her how much the sets cost. She gazed at them, rich and heart colored. Peerless as a peace offering. After a moment she told the butcher she'd take a single set. She would present it to Jack that night for dinner, and tell him it was a miracle.

In high spirits Iris sped through the store, escaping unnoticed until she made it to the parking lot, where she was unloading groceries—gently, trying to spare her back—when the sound of a wheelchair motor burred in her ear. "If it isn't the talk of the town," Kay Wendell said.

Iris let the groceries in her hands drop. "Kay. What a surprise."

"Do you know what people are saying?"

"I feel like I have to go out with a bag over my head." She smiled, but Kay refused to be drawn in.

"The parish is half lunatic about this. Six people have told me that you're performing miracles."

"Well, Kay, you know—people." Kay was squinting, her face twisted and wild, and Iris edged back.

"What really happened?"

"There was more food than we thought. We wound up being able to feed the patients. We were all glad." Iris squeezed her mouth into a smile.

"People are acting like it's the second coming."

"That's not my doing. But it's surprising that one little ham could go so far."

"So you're calling this divine intervention." Kay snickered.

"I'm not calling it anything." Iris stretched out her hand to brush back hair from Kay's eyes, but the other woman was already turning and chugging away. "Don't try to touch me. Do you think I'm waiting for a miracle? I know what to expect from the world," Kay called over her shoulder.

It occurred to Iris that this was Kay's whole problem, and she was irritated enough to catch up and tell her so. As Iris hurried behind the chair, Kay snapped at her. "Get away from me. I'm not looking for your grubby cures. Get away!" She flapped her hands at Iris, who stopped the chair, caught Kay's frail wrists in one hand, the top of her skull with the other, and bore down. "I've never known anyone who deserved curing more," Iris said, twisting Kay's wrists a little.

Kay stopped struggling, and in its sudden collapse her body seemed even tinier. "Go on, then," she said. "Make me dance."

"It's not so easy—" Iris began.

"I know, walk a mile in your shoes. Well, Mrs. Miracle Worker, I wouldn't mind trading in my shoes for yours."

"Fine," Iris said, and picked Kay up out of her chair before she had any idea what to do with her. The woman was heavier than she looked, and Iris staggered, shoving Kay onto the hood of a station wagon before her own legs folded and she dropped into Kay's chair.

"Am I supposed to walk to you? You must have gotten some of the mumbo wrong." Kay pointed to her flaccid legs. "They still don't work."

"Fine," said Iris again, examining the switches on the arm of the chair. "You stay put. I'm just going to put on your shoes here."

"You idiot," Kay snarled. "It's not a Disneyland ride."

But it might as well have been; Iris found the lever to lift the brake, then turned and whirred up the slight incline of the parking lot, away from Kay.

"You'll burn the motor out!" Kay yelled. "Are you planning to take care of me when it's broken?" Iris leaned forward in the chair to urge it along. She felt pleasantly mischievous. When she came to a speed bump she had to take two runs before the chair cleared it, making a harsh, mechanical cough. It stopped on the other side. Kay was squalling from the station wagon, attracting attention. To get away, Iris nudged the lever; the engine coughed again but the chair only slid back an inch, settling at the speed bump.

"See?" Kay was shrieking. "*See?*" Iris jabbed at the switches, but the little motor whined, the sound all wrong. "Please," Iris muttered, knowing already she was done for. "Damn."

Exhaling unevenly, she tried to stand, to wheel the chair back to Kay and face the music. It was then that her back, dazzling with pain, seized Iris so she gasped, unable to move. She looked up to see Kay crying and waving her arms. Iris was crying herself; hot blades seemed to be carving channels on either side of her spine. She knew she needed to reach Kay, who would get help. But she couldn't move, and had to watch Kay screaming and pointing at her before people finally came out from the store to save them.

BLUE SKIES

Constance didn't know why she was watching Ray. He came home right after work; he ate with good appetite. He set out a garden as a thank-you gift to her for staying through the first angry months he was on the wagon. Weekends he helped her dig.

The garden was the first she'd had since she'd run off to marry him, and even in their strangled backyard soil, packed too hard and seamed with pebbles and old mortar, she was able to grow plants she'd never had any success with. Pea plants launched themselves against the back fence, and the strawberry runners formed a solid carpet over the ground, dense as matting. Now she had ambitions for corn, too, if she could get Ray to till the space on the west side of the house.

After dinner, when she watered, Ray leaned on a hoe and talked to her. These days he loved to talk. He told her about work, hauling onions down to Modesto or Vacaville, troubles with the shipments, jokes he'd heard on his CB. He met her eye and sang her the corny country songs he listened to all day.

"Send me the pillow that you dream on, so darlin', I can dream on it, too," he yodeled while she tugged at a broadleaf root as thick as his finger.

Still she couldn't help herself. She watched him while he dressed in the mornings, the way he tiptoed to keep from waking her. She watched him nap on Sunday afternoons and stooped to inhale his breath, sour from 7-Up and coffee. She began to inventory the house, checking behind the towels and in the garage. Three years before, when he'd been arrested for DUI in Nashville, she found bottles stashed in the garment bag with his wedding suit. Now his eyes were clear and she found no bottles at all, but she only looked harder.

She was ashamed of what she was doing, and prayed to overcome the demons of doubt. She hated to think how hurt Ray would be if he knew that only last week she had quietly driven to the yard and tailed him all the way home—where he came directly, observing posted speed limits and signaling well in advance of his turns. When Constance pulled into the driveway, he turned, delighted. "Were you right behind me, angel? I didn't even see you!"

Angel. It was something Ray had picked up from his country songs. She'd already told him she didn't like it, but in the mornings, before he went to work, he would come up behind her and cradle her shoulders in his ropy arms. "My angel of light. My guardian angel."

"Your angel needs to know what you want for dinner," she said one morning in June. He'd been sober almost six months.

"Strawberries," he said, sliding his hands down her sides. "Our harvest."

"You wanted our harvest night before last to put on your

ice cream. You expect more than that poor garden can put out."

"If you don't have expectations, nothing can live up to them," he said, bending to gnaw at the top of her ear.

Constance ducked away and planned a pot roast. She had read somewhere that nutrition was important to sobriety, and ever since she'd been packing Ray's lunch with extra sandwiches and bananas.

She dawdled, lingering until Ray kissed her good-bye and whistled out the door. Then she hurried into the bedroom and stood in front of the closet, pressing her face against every one of his shirts in turn, checking for the stale cigarette smell that would mean he had been to a bar. She didn't stop until she got to his best white shirt, which she knew good and well he hadn't worn since their neighbor Judy's wedding.

Leaning into the closet, her face pressed against the stiff cloth, Constance began to cry. She and Ray had been married six years, and more than five of them had been grubby and desperate, years spent begging landlords for extensions and facing dinners of macaroni and potatoes. Now they had lived eight months in Rushdale, Ray hadn't missed a day of work, and Constance felt as if she'd been slammed onto dry land after a long storm. But she couldn't forget the feeling of treacherous swells beneath her feet.

At ten that morning, after Constance had washed the breakfast dishes and made up the bed, Ray called. He had never called her from work before, and his voice sounded so hushed and thin that it took her a minute to recognize him.

"Hi, angel. You already cleaned those strawberries?"

"What's wrong?"

"Not a thing in the world. Nothin' but blue skies. You started dinner already?"

"I haven't even washed my face yet."

"What do you say I take you out tonight? Wine you and dine you."

"What are you saying, Ray?" Constance said, alarmed now and craning over the phone as if she could grab hold of him that way.

He giggled. "Just a figure of speech. Come on, girl. Take today off and have a milk bath. We can have a date. Let me take you out to dinner and this weekend I'll make a trellis for your peas. They're a mess."

Constance shook her head. "Would you like me to give you a list of every bill we haven't paid off?"

"The Lord never meant for us to use all our money just to pay bills."

"How would you know? You haven't been in a church in twenty years," she said.

"Heard it on the radio. See you tonight, dollface."

It took Constance a minute after he hung up to realize she was panting like a dog, the old, nauseating dread rolling in her stomach. She slipped her shoes on and gathered the spade and weeder and bucket she kept next to the back door.

It had been a heavy morning, the sun late in burning off the fog, so the soil in the bed was still moist and the air smelled sweet. Arrested, she stared at the garden as if she'd never seen it before—the tender nests of lettuce, the strings of yellow and white blossoms on the peas. The air was hot already, stitched in with the cries of mockingbirds drawn to the rich, rotted strawberries. She dropped to her knees and brushed her cheek with a hairy zucchini leaf. She ate the leaf right off the vine, snapping its tough stem between her front teeth and chewing even though the bitter, grassy taste made her eyes water. Her thigh grazed the tender pepper leaves, just unfurling—they were Ray's favorite, and she had already promised to make pepper stew with the first crop. She touched the dark leaf with the tips of her fingers. If he started to drink again, she would plow every one of them under.

To her relief, Ray took Constance to The Door of Italy, a modest restaurant that catered to families, and he waved away the waitress who asked if they would like wine. All around them couples were nodding and murmuring. "Judy says to watch out for whiteflies on the tomatoes. She says whiteflies are the big killer around here," Constance said while Ray whistled softly into the menu. "I check the plants, but I don't know what else to do."

Ray smiled and reached across the table to hold her hand. "You keep a good eye on things."

"I'm just trying for damage containment. The zucchini vines are already a yard long, and they haven't even set blossom yet."

"I like to see you happy," Ray said.

"I'm a lark," Constance muttered, watching his thumb scrape over her knuckles.

"You deserve it, after all the rough times."

"Where do you suppose that waitress is? I'm ready for my salad."

"What's wrong, angel?"

Constance pulled back her hand. "I'm happy. I sing all day. I just don't like to push my luck."

"The way I figure, you're owed, plus overtime." He cleared his throat. "I have some news," he said. He was watching, waiting for her to smile, but Constance felt dread washing over her. "You'll never believe who came to see me today: Monty George."

Constance put down the glass. "Christ almighty."

"No, wait," Ray chuckled. "It was great—he snuck into my cab. He was waiting there for me when I signed out of the office. He started laughing so hard when he saw the look on my face, he about fell out."

"How did he know where you were?" Constance asked.

"He happened to be in town, and he saw me driving out last week, so he waited until he could catch me."

"He just happened to be in Rushdale? Just looking for life to happen in Rushdale, California?"

"He's changed. He's a distributor for AgPro. He was in town with a new line."

"Monty has become a salesman?"

"I told you he's changed."

Constance tried to drink her water, but her throat was hard and tight. Ray had never been able to lie to her, often as he'd tried when he was drinking. She'd known from the second he phoned that morning. But for all the time spent sniffing Ray's shirts, she was still caught unawares. She could never have sniffed out Monty.

"—and damn if he doesn't tell me that he's sober, too!" Ray was saying. "He's got me beat by thirteen months. The day the cop had to tell him what city he was in, he began to consider adjustments." Ray whooped and slapped his thigh.

"What does he want?"

Ray wiped his eyes. "He wants to see you, for one thing. He asked about you right off."

"Don't tell me that Monty George snuck into your truck because he wanted to know about me."

"You'll be surprised when you see him. He said he had an idea, but he didn't want to talk about it unless you were there, too. He still talks the same way. Any partnership, he said, requires full communication."

Constance was rolling shreds of her bread into pellets. "What do you suppose he meant by that?"

"I think he has an idea, angel," Ray said, bending swiftly to kiss her hand and then gesturing to the waitress.

Monty dated back to Cleveland, and the long-distance refrigeration company that had work for Ray one week out of three. Constance and Ray had been married just over a year, long enough for their positions to harden; their arguing was daily and mean. Monty lived downstairs and knocked on the door their first morning there. Constance was twenty-two, still capable of hope. She let him in.

He was half a head shorter than she, a tiny man. By the summer, when she would awaken to find him watching their television, she would come to know the fragile length of his shin, and his shoulders, as undeveloped as a boy's. But on this first icy day, all she noticed was the sheen his skin gave off, as if it held too much blood.

"So you're the new footsteps," he said. "You walk a lot— did anyone ever tell you that?"

It was a Saturday, and Ray was still in bed, snoring through slack lips. "My husband is in the other room," she said. "We only came yesterday, from Indiana."

Monty pushed past her, glancing into the galley where she had piled their three boxes of dishes and pots, and pausing at the sheet she had tacked to the ceiling to separate the bed from the rest of the room. "Are you going to be making breakfast soon?" he said. "I'd like to know what your schedule is, as long as I'm going to be hearing you anyway. Myself, I'm an early bird. Hate to miss the dawn." He scooted back to Constance and rested his pudgy hand on her wrist. "You never know when life is going to happen."

As if on cue, Constance heard Ray swing his feet to the floor. He shambled out from behind the sheet, blinking into the light like a bear. "Think you could get it any colder in here, Constance?" he said. He held the blanket around him for a robe, and she could smell his breath from where she stood.

"This is Monty. He lives downstairs."

Ray squinted at him. "You're the little guy who watched me pull the mattress up the stairs."

"I'm not much help," Monty said with a shrug. "Best to stay out of the way. Why don't you come on down to my place? I've got something that can warm you up." He winked.

Ray lifted his head then and looked sharply at Monty. "I believe," he said, "I'll do that. Neighborly."

"Neighborly," Monty repeated, and bowed to him, his arms at his side and his tight body creasing at the waist.

Constance said, "I believe I'll stay. I won't be comfortable until things are tidy." But Ray and Monty were bowing toward each other like dolls, grinning and repeating, "I will. I believe I'll do that, neighbor." After they went downstairs she made a point of walking across the apartment as many times as she could, stamping her feet over the place where she judged Monty's sofa might be.

Ray didn't come home until after nine. Constance had lined the kitchen cupboard and put all the dishes away, hung and folded her clothes. At seven she heated up a pot of soup, and at seven-thirty dumped the remainder down the drain, scrubbed and put away the pot and her bowl and spoon. When Ray came in she was reading an article about cupcakes in a year-old *Woman's Day* she'd found in the closet.

"Do you know what you sound like from downstairs?" he asked her from the doorway.

"What if you get called to work tomorrow?" she said.

Ray minced across the floor, lifting his knees waist high on each step, then furiously drumming his feet when he reached the middle of the room. "You sound just like that. A hundred pound mouse."

"The dispatcher could call, you know. They fill most of their replacements on Monday."

"Stop mousing at me, woman," he said, and giggled.

"'We'll go to Cleveland,'" she mimicked. "'Lots of trucking firms there. You'll see—it was just a run of bad luck.'"

"Squeak, squeak, squeak. Sorry, Constance, but I can't hear you over all the mice in here."

"It doesn't take you long, does it?" she said.

"I have the gift for making friends."

"If you could just *hear* yourself."

Ray's expression softened, then collapsed into tragic remorse; he dropped his hands and sat on the box beside him, which crumpled under his weight. Looking up at her from the floor he said, "It's not fair, is it? You were up here all day by yourself, putting things away. I got to have fun while you were putting things away."

"It's all right," Constance said. "I got a lot done."

"No, it's *not* all right. You're my wife. You shouldn't have to be alone all day. Tomorrow I'll tell Monty to come up here."

"Ray, for God's sake."

He stood up and waved his hands; he would hear no more. "And if we see any mice," he said before he pulled down the sheet to the alcove, "we'll shoot them."

Like Ray, Monty was a happy drunk. In the whole year they lived in Cleveland, Constance never saw him fully sober. But the more Monty drank, the more courtly he became, and the more apt to share his delight over a sunrise, new irises in the spring, Constance's hamburger casserole. When she brought in clean laundry he buried his face in it and cried, "Just smell! Clean sheets!" He'd pound his tiny fist against the wall.

Constance hadn't encouraged him, but still Monty marveled at every counter she sponged, every baked potato. Eventually her impatience and embarrassment dropped away, and she found herself pointing out bellying clouds just so she could watch how his ears reddened when he was excited. When she prepared dinner he hoisted himself onto the narrow counter and narrated her actions.

"She's chopping up the onions now; her knife's a blur. She goes so fast she doesn't have a chance to cry. Now she's checking the bowl with the bread dough, seeing how it's rising. It's rising like the sun. And now she's back to the cutting board with more onions."

From the outer room Ray would wander in, rummage in the tiny refrigerator, and pull out two cans. In all the time he spent with them, Monty never helped himself. Ray would pause until Monty picked up his narration again, and then return to the upholstered chair left by the previous tenant. They would stay up long after Constance went to bed; she learned to fall asleep through their giggling and proclamations. Often as not, Constance found Ray passed out in his chair in the morning, but Monty was awake and ready for her, full of details about what she'd missed.

She had no idea how he lived. At least Ray drove occasionally, bringing home enough for potatoes and another week's rent. But she never saw Monty work. Sometimes, when she reminded him that he ate all his meals with them and used their squat shower, he would pull a damp twenty-dollar bill from his shirt pocket. Constance always took it, too embarrassed to ask where the money came from.

In October, a week after the quarrel with his supervisor that cut Ray off forever from Cleveland Refrigerated Hauling, Constance had snapped awake in the middle of the night. The towel over the window had slipped, and the grayish moonlight was bright enough to read by. As she stood on the bed to rehang the towel, she heard something from the outer room—a dim, blurred sound—and she realized now that it had been going on for some time. Constance steadied herself against the window and listened. This was nothing like Ray and Monty's usual uproar, the nights they spent singing chorus after chorus of "Blue Skies." The sound was murmurous and steady as a pulse.

She edged off the bed next to the sheet, pulling up the corner just enough to see into the outer room. Ray and Monty were sitting on the floor, their legs crossed. A candle burned between them with thick braids of wax collapsing down its sides. The wick had sunk so that it gave off almost no light, and she couldn't see Ray's expression, but Monty's, just over the flame, was rapt, his little, pie-shaped face wet and shining. "Full moon," he said. "Full moon. Fill up my pockets."

"Full moon, full moon. Fill up my pockets," Ray joined him. He was swaying slightly.

Constance could see that her pots and bowls were on the floor around the two men, even the good cut-glass bowl that she had forbidden Ray ever to touch. "What are you *doing?*" she cried, and Ray's voice faltered when he looked up. Monty kept chanting, glancing away from the candle only long enough to nod at her.

"Hey, Constance. You ought to like this. We are bringing home the bacon," Ray said, swallowing a belch.

"Hush," Monty said serenely. "We're almost finished. Full moon, full moon, fill up my pockets."

Constance leaned against the wall and watched while Monty and her husband chanted, surrounded by open bowls. Their voices swelled and subsided like waves. "Ray, for God's sake," she said.

Monty rose to his feet and raised his palms toward the ceiling. "Full moon!" he cried. "Full moon! Fill up my pockets! Fill! Fill! Fill!"

Ray stood, too, and gazed at the ceiling as if he expected to see faces there. "Fill! Fill! Fill!"

For a moment they held their positions in attentive silence. Then Monty dropped his arms and shrugged, massaging his shoulder. "Now we wait," he said to Ray.

"I told you she'd be like this," Ray said, motioning with his head to Constance.

"Aren't you two a little old for seances?" she asked.

Monty looked modestly at the floor. Ray said, "You don't even know what you're seeing. This is power. This is putting ourselves in the center of life's ongoing process."

"The only thing you're in the center of is a bottle. Full moon. I came up with better magic in grade school."

"That's your whole problem, Constance. We're calling on the power of the whole damn beautiful universe, and you want to sleep through it."

"I must have missed the part with the universe. By the time you woke me up, all that was going on was two drunks howling at the moon."

Monty shook his head. "It's a shame."

Constance glared at him. "This is all you, isn't it? This was your brilliant idea."

He shrugged again. "I do it every month. Once I opened a drawer and found a hundred and sixty-four dollars."

"A hundred sixty-four dollars!" Ray broke in. "For opening a drawer! And he never has to put up with snide sons of bitches who think they can tell me how to drive my own route."

"Out," Constance said to Monty, pointing to the door.

"He's only telling you the truth. If you'd just open your eyes, you could be happy," Monty said.

She grabbed Monty at the elbow, her fingers sinking into the fleshy joint. "Every time I open my eyes, you've caused more damage. We came here to start fresh, but you've made him worse than ever."

"He's my friend. You can't talk like that to my friend," Ray said, but he had slumped into the chair, one foot propped on her soup pot, and his head wobbled and drooped.

"You don't know what you're doing. I want to help you. I'm your best friend," Monty said to Constance, who was marching him to the door.

"I'll know my friends when I meet them," she said. "You can bet they won't be sponging little drunks who expect miracles to pay their rent." She yanked him into the hall, where the light was out again, and shoved him in the direction of the stairs. After she heard the soft thump of his body hitting a wall, she closed her apartment door, blew out the guttering candle flame, and went back to bed, pulling the blanket over her head to block out Ray's snoring, a sound Monty had once called magnificent.

On the way home from The Door of Italy Constance was quiet, smiling at Ray's jokes, reaching across the seat to squeeze his hand when he told her how pretty she looked. As soon as he left the house the next morning—a long day ahead, a full load from Salinas—she headed for the shower. Constance knew she needed to get to Monty first. She couldn't wait for Ray to bring him home; already she could imagine the two of them at the door, giggling and bowing. She had to brace herself against the shower wall at the thought.

Just as she was leaving, she picked up a sack and hurried out to the garden. She collected five firm lettuce heads and a handful of snow peas, glancing at the tomato plants while she picked. If she had to make small talk, she could always ask him about whiteflies.

It was a clear day, still cool in the shade. Constance found herself half-jogging, and she jumped when a dog yapped at her. Now that she knew he was here, she expected Monty to pounce on her from behind every tree, and before she was five blocks from home, her heart was already thudding. She had to pause in a doorway to smooth her hair and skirt, and even so she was breathless when she walked into the beige waiting room and the receptionist looked up.

"Monty George," Constance said, and a man standing at the filing cabinet turned and grinned.

"I knew I knew those footsteps. How are you, Constance?"

"Good Lord," she said. He had become slim and lithe. She could have passed him on the street without looking twice. His dark slacks hung with a snappy crease, and rich hair waved over his forehead. He reminded Constance of a politician.

"You still have a call waiting, Mr. Miller," the receptionist said, and Constance glanced around.

"I'll call back," Monty said, crossing the room and touching Constance just above the elbow.

"Mr. Miller?" Constance said.

"The name my father gave me. Once I got sober, I thought I should respect it."

"Ray didn't mention you had a new name."

"I didn't have time to tell him." He winked up at her.

"Things don't change, do they? You always did know more about me than Ray."

"I don't know about that," Constance murmured, then held out the sack of vegetables. "They're from our garden. Ray set it out for me."

"He mentioned," Monty said. "He said that you could make anything grow."

"He exaggerates," she said. "You know Ray."

"Not anymore. He looks great, Constance. You've been good for him." She shrugged, but Monty pressed his hand, now lean as a fish, back on her elbow and kept talking. "I love how life brings the loose ends back together. After all those years ago in that dump in Cleveland, here we are in California. And looking better for the journey. So, are you going to join us for lunch?"

Constance had been distracted by the weight of his hand on her arm; the question caught her off balance. "Lunch?"

"Isn't that why you're here? I'm supposed to meet Ray in ten minutes."

"Ray's driving to Salinas. He won't be back until late."

"His routing got changed this morning. Just a run to the extension office. He probably tried to call you, but you were already out." He smiled, told the receptionist they would be back in two hours, and propelled Constance out the door while she stammered and hesitated. The last twosome on earth she wanted to join was Ray and Monty.

The sunlight was sharp, and she squinted at Monty, realizing she'd never seen him outside before. He walked with an assertive slide; Constance saw women across the street cut their eyes to him. He was telling stories, bouncing on the balls of his feet, hurrying her like a terrier. She wouldn't believe the coincidences in his life since he'd stopped drinking. He'd met people he hadn't seen since he was a boy. What he'd finally learned was that paths were set up to cross and cross again. So much needless anxiety. We never really lost anybody.

He steered her around the corner and across two streets, calling out to people as they went. He could greet them by name, remember children and pets. "How'd those onions take to the new manure?" he yelled. "Ever find Scooter's doll?"

He chattered and whooped all the way into The Happy Cup, where Ray, waiting with coffee, jumped up as Constance came in.

"Look who found me this morning," Monty said, nudging Constance to sit down and then crowding in next to her.

Ray relaxed, smiling at her frown and slinging his arm across the back of the seat. "This is great. So much to catch up on."

"Do you have a self-respecting refrigerator yet? I remember Constance defrosting the one in Cleveland every other day."

Constance glanced at Monty with surprise. She thought she remembered every inch of that apartment, but she had forgotten the refrigerator. Monty had named it Juneau.

"And that godawful *chair*," Ray was saying. "Every time you sat down your head was level with your knees."

Monty shook his head in delight. "One night after you went to bed I was wide awake and hungry, so I took a box of macaroni and cheese, ran water into a bowl, and just dumped everything in. I figured the macaroni would soften up eventually, but after ten minutes they were still like little u-joints. I knew Constance would get mad if she found it in the trash, so I took the whole pot up on the roof and spread the stuff around like roofing tar. That orange sauce reflected the moon-light, and I got inspired. I dribbled it out to spell 'WE.' I wanted to do 'WELCOME,' but I ran out."

Constance rolled her eyes, but Ray was laughing so hard he had to clutch the table. "I saw that," he finally gasped. "I went up one night to drink and I saw this weird fuzzy patch out by the edge. I was afraid to get near it. It looked radio-active."

"Do you remember anything?" Monty asked, wheeling to face Constance, who shuddered.

"I'm not like you. I try to forget." In her dreams, when Ray started drinking again, it was always this apartment she re-turned to. "I could never get the kitchen clean."

"I remember Monty sitting on the counter and singing 'She'll Be Comin' 'Round the Mountain' while you made din-ner," Ray said. "I never heard so many verses."

"I'm surprised we can remember anything," Monty yipped.

"Me, too," said Constance sourly, and the two men laughed harder, Ray reaching for her hand while Monty snaked his short arm around her shoulders.

"Who would have *guessed?*" Ray said. "Who would have ever imagined we'd survive it?"

Constance cleared her throat. "So, Monty. What can you tell me about whiteflies?"

He sat up again, affectionately squeezing her shoulder be-fore he let his arm slip. "We have some products I can sample for you, but"—he glanced around and lowered his voice—"I'll tell you the best thing. Garlic spray, a little patience. And grow marigolds. They repel bugs, and look cheerful in the garden."

Constance frowned. "I want to have tomatoes *this* year."

"You should see her in that garden," Ray said. "If a plant doesn't come up, it's got Constance to answer to."

"I'd come up," Monty said.

"Me, too," said Ray.

"Broccoli's more obedient than you two ever were," Constance said.

Ray leaned toward Monty. "She keeps that broccoli running on time." He lifted his eyebrows, the look he always used to encourage her. She didn't feel encouraged. She felt as though she were in a room with no air.

"Sorry," she said, trying to sound light. "All I asked about was whiteflies."

The three of them stopped talking, and in the pause Constance saw Ray's crestfallen look and a spot that had somehow gotten on his shirt since the morning. She dropped her eyes. She hadn't meant to sound so hard. They pushed her; they always had. "Maybe you don't need marigolds," Monty was saying. "Those snow peas you brought me look fine. And of course there are several products."

"No, you're right," she said, cutting Monty off. "I'll try them. Who knows? Couldn't hurt."

"Couldn't hurt," said Ray, brightening.

"Who knows?" said Monty.

Constance left Ray and Monty at the café. They wheedled and protested when she got up, but by the time she made it to the door they had their elbows on the table and were snorting like a couple of teenagers. Ray came home that night with marigold flats balanced on each arm.

"Monty really knows about this," he said over dinner. "He's been reading up, talking to people, visiting organic farms. You should hear it. Interplanting, pheromones."

"I'll bet he plants at high tide, too." Constance speared a piece of pot roast for Ray's plate.

"Monty never met an idea he couldn't improve on. The man's got vision. Doesn't he look great?"

Constance sighed. "No. Maybe. I don't know what to think. He doesn't look like the same person. He doesn't even have the same name."

"Give him a chance. The sin but not the sinner, right?"

"I'm trying," Constance muttered, staring at her plate.

"Don't try so hard, angel." Ray lifted his eyebrows and smiled crookedly at her.

She shook her head. "So, did you stay in The Happy Cup all afternoon?"

"We went for a drive—he wanted to show me the acreage he's leased east of town. People waved when we passed. I felt like I was with a movie star."

"He may have missed his calling. How was the land?"

"What do I know? He's got forty acres. He wanted to know if a truck could get through for pickups."

"Forty acres?" Constance said. "How does he think he's going to live? You can't even get grocery money off forty acres."

Ray hunched forward and pushed his plate away. "He figures on staying with AgPro. He wants to try some ideas, that's all."

"Good luck to him. Cultivating that kind of land and holding down a job ought to wear out even Monty George."

"It's leveled, already prepared," Ray said. "He wants to raise different crops, some things that are new around here. Work by hand. Get someone he trusts to work with him." Ray stopped and looked at Constance, who practically choked.

"Oh, no," she said. "Sorry, boys. I'll wait for the moon to fill up my pockets before I tenant for Monty George."

"Stop for a minute and listen. You'd finally have enough room to grow corn. And Monty's got strategies for the rust you were getting on that lettuce."

"So you two just sat there all afternoon and planned my future."

"He's got you in mind. He thinks you're what the whole idea needs."

"What, somebody sober?" Constance cried, and Ray set his mouth. "Or somebody who knows how to work? You think everything has changed. Well, nothing's changed. You and Monty George talk, and I'm the one who does the hoeing."

"You know," he said, his voice so high and tight it seemed to curl at the edges, "that's exactly what Monty said. 'Somebody has to be sober here.' His words exactly."

"How reassuring, to hear Monty's assessment of the situation."

"You'd be in real danger of learning something if you stopped your precious work long enough to listen."

"You'd be in danger of making something of yourself if you'd quit listening to Monty. Or maybe you'd rather be up on the roof with macaroni and cheese."

"People do change, Constance. But you sit there and count up every mistake."

"Are we calling five and a half years a mistake?" Looking at Ray's bland, satisfied face, she had to clutch the edge of the table. "We didn't have *heat*, dammit. I slept next to you after I cleaned up your vomit. Am I supposed to believe you've changed just like that?"

Ray shook his head, his lips thin and trembling. "That's right. You pinned it. You're supposed to believe I've changed just like that." He pushed his chair back from the table.

"Where are you going?" she said, watching him move toward the door and pick up his jacket.

"Guess."

He let the screen door bang behind him, and Constance watched from the kitchen table as he skirted the garden and jumped lightly over the fence. She was shaking and couldn't catch her breath. She hadn't heard that spiny threat in Ray's voice in six months; it was almost thrilling.

After five minutes she got up to clear the table, her arms still trembling. She wished he'd eaten more dinner. She wished he'd stayed long enough to let her tell him he was a saint. Anyone could see it. But she was a saint, too, and she was ready to hear somebody say so.

At ten o'clock, when Ray wasn't back, Constance couldn't stand waiting anymore and went out walking. She knew where to go. During their first week in town she had made note of the bars, judging the ones most likely to have a country-western jukebox and a sing-along clintele. She tried First Call on Fourth Street, Arlene's on Dixon. No Ray, no Monty. She walked twice past The Long Stop, down from Arlene's, but a brassy din bellied out the door and she couldn't force herself into it.

Instead she wandered back home, where she knew Ray wouldn't be waiting for her. It was a comforting thought, and Constance relaxed as the sweet night air settled on her arms. She could glimpse other people's gardens by the occasional porch light—shapes of trees and hedges, white roses like candles in the dark. Passing a low fence draped with honeysuckle, Constance picked off a strand to smell as she walked.

By the time she turned onto her block, she felt buoyant, ready for a drive. It wasn't Ray she wanted to find, but the land itself. The creamy moon was finally rising, giving Constance enough light once she was out of town to see where to turn off the state road, and then off the gravel access spur, and then to make out the two figures alone in the fields, standing and waving her in.

"Took you long enough," Ray said when she closed the car door behind her. "I didn't think you were coming, but Monty kept saying we had to wait for you."

"What are you waiting for?" Constance said, teetering and sliding down the low incline toward them.

"Balance," Monty said. "Root, stem, leaf."

"Don't tell me," Constance said. "I get to be the root."

"You hold things in place, angel," Ray said.

"All our searching brought us here," said Monty, and she turned to him.

"You didn't have to search us out," she said. "We were doing fine."

"Life puts us in each other's way," he murmured.

"I'm ready to be in someone else's way," she said.

"Then why did you come here tonight?" asked Ray.

"To serve notice," she said.

During the long pause that followed she listened to the night insects and felt pleasantly airborne. "Constance?" Ray finally said, his voice jagged. "Are you going to leave now? After everything?"

"I could use a break," she said after a while.

A week later, she rode back out to the plot with Ray and Monty. They rode in Ray's cab, Constance sitting up high between the two men, who kept laughing and elbowing across her to switch the radio stations.

In the daylight she could see that the plot was hedged on two sides by walnut groves. Constance wondered about late-afternoon shadows, but she kept her concern to herself. Beside her, Monty was craning to see over the dashboard. He pointed out the places he had retilled, where the soil lay like cake in dark and moist ridges.

The men got out of the truck and Monty began to pace out rows, marking with twine. From the co-op he had brought compost and seed in bulk. Constance poured herself a cup of coffee from Ray's thermos, sat on the cab's step, and watched them. She smiled, waved, and stayed put whenever they called to her.

They clowned, hurdling the furrows and pitching face-down at the end of every row. Sometimes they came back to the truck and double-checked the graphs Monty had brought. Constance sat and watched, trying to envision Monty's curving rows of chard, his rye and squash side by side. She should have known Monty's garden would be like no one else's. Even when she could see they were getting it wrong— the rows too close, seeds too shallow—she smiled and waved to them, and didn't say a word.

RICH

At nine-fifteen Larry went ahead and started closing out the register. He turned up the music to cover the embarrassing quiet, and the one guy who'd been drinking wine coolers all night started singing along, motioning Larry to join him. Larry grinned cheesily. Nights like this he remembered the stories he'd read as a kid about Houdini wrapped in chains, locked in a chest, dropped overboard. Ignoring his waitress Dana Evans's smile and her breasts shoved up next to his arm, he recounted the night's take. Kit would be sure to ask.

Kit was on the phone when he came home, her heels propped next to the open window, and she was smoking, though she'd promised to stop. She smiled as he came in and made a face at her cigarette, then dragged the phone into the closet-sized extra room where they kept boxes they still hadn't unpacked. This meant she was talking to her parents, and the conversation could go on another hour.

He went for the pot of coffee she had left on the burner, listening for anything that might slide out from under the door.

He hadn't met her parents, although he and Kit had been married six months; Kit had hardly let him greet them over the phone. "Are they missing important limbs? Do they drool?" he would ask, dogging around after her. Larry's own parents had died years before, and he had a yearning now for the safe enclosure of family. "We could go visit them for a weekend."

Kit twined herself around him, starting at the knees. "I have another idea for the weekend," she whispered, and he lost track of his thinking.

But he brought the subject back up when it occurred to him, often in the mornings when she was getting dressed for work. "What does your old man do, anyway?"

"He's retired," she said, whacking cigarette ashes and pizza crumbs off the bedside table.

"What did he do? If it isn't a national secret."

"Trade." She dimpled at him, so coyly cute he laughed and let her win. He sometimes remembered the scene as he sat in his restaurant, waiting for a customer.

Now he was on his second cup of coffee, nursing a dull headache, and she sidled back into the kitchen. Her round face shone, traces of a smile still lingering around her mouth. "I didn't expect you home so soon," she said.

"Things keep up like this, you'll be seeing me on a full-time basis. Barely two hundred."

"It's a Tuesday. You can't expect a crowd on a Tuesday."

"After expenses, we cleared four bucks."

She sighed. "Give yourself a chance. Things will turn around. Everybody likes to eat out."

"You don't," he reminded her.

"I've seen what happens to food out there in the world," she said, bending to kiss him lightly on the hair. "You can't go under. You still have two years on your lease."

"A helpful reminder," he said grimly, and then, "I don't know what else I can do. Have a drawing and force the winner to come and eat?"

"Word will get around. You'll have customers before you know it." She moved to the sink, where dishes were piled up, and jerked the hot water on hard.

Larry set down his coffee cup at the edge of the table. "Turn that off and sit here with me, all right? Cheer me up. Tell me"—he issued a tense smile as she turned off the water— "how your day went. What did your folks have to say?"

"Oh, family stuff," she said, perching on a chair. "Listen, Lyle had a new joke today: Man stands looking out the window at a dog licking its privates. Man says to his friend, 'My God, that looks wonderful. I wish I could do that.' Friend looks at him and shrugs. 'Well, it's your dog.'"

"Kit, that's a million years old," he said while she hugged herself and half collapsed in laughter.

"It's a great joke," she gasped, pounding the table so hard she knocked his cup of steaming coffee to the floor. It splashed his leg from knee to ankle, and he howled.

"Larry, I'm *sorry*. Quick, take your pants off. That hurts to look at," she said, going for paper towels. Larry rocked back and forth and sucked his teeth, feeling fat weals already bubbling on his ankle.

"Get me some ice," he moaned, and Kit shook her head, rummaging in the cupboard for the yellow baking soda box.

"This is better. Takes out the sting and doesn't leave a scar."

"Christ, Kit, I didn't ask your opinion." He scooted across the floor and reached into the freezer himself, his leg shimmering with pain.

"I'm sorry," she said flatly.

"I just wish you'd be careful. You aren't careful," he said, trying to hold the ice cubes in place with both hands.

"I'm sorry," she said, and he knew he was making her miserable, but he couldn't stop. "I needed a little help tonight, can you understand that? A little comfort."

"What can I do?" she whispered.

He paused, considering. Buy out the restaurant? Let him have a week in Tahiti with Dana? "Introduce me to your parents," he said, and watched, amazed, as she shuddered against the counter. "Come on, girl. It won't be as bad as all that."

"You can't imagine," she said.

By midnight, when Kit went to bed, chains of furious white blisters fanned up Larry's shin. He found some relief sitting in a tub of ice water, but ten minutes after he got out, his leg was stinging again, the tight blisters on the bone already starting to blaze.

He installed himself in front of the TV with bags of ice draped gingerly over his leg, a water glass, scotch, and aspirin on the table beside him. Although he wished he could stop, he still blamed Kit. She had a perversity of timing that was brilliant—waltzing into the restaurant the one night Dana wore a blouse that was practically sheer, or waiting until he was melancholy with drink before calling him lightly to the bedroom. They never seemed to be running at the same speed, and he wondered if all new couples spent so much time apologizing—for her huge practical jokes, for his long glooms. The apologies went back and forth like Ping-Pong balls until Larry was finally reduced to apologizing again for having believed, in the lunatic moment that never wholly left them, that he wanted to leave her.

"It's over. It's done. We're moving ahead." She would stroke his damp hair while he kicked off the sheet, unconsoled, crying a little. "How can you expect me to believe that?" he'd ask.

"I've never lied to you." But something made him watchful—something in her crossed arms, the tilt of her neck. Meanwhile, he apologized again, promising to believe her. He owed her that much. He owed her more than that. His marriage, not even a year old, felt like a solid page of debt.

Shifting now on the chair, trying to balance the bags of ice, he reflected that he would have been slower to propose if he'd known marriage would involve so many balance sheets. Larry and Kit had tumbled into love as if into a well, darting across the width of Elite, Indiana, where she'd come to manage the Thriftway, licking each other's fingers on lunch breaks, stealing into each other's cars. One night when Larry had to stay late, closing accounts at the restaurant, Kit crawled into his office and began by unlacing his shoes. Larry, startled, cried out, but she shushed him with a sound like a growl and he didn't make another noise until she had taken away all of his clothes and straddled him in his chair.

A month later they were talking marriage and Kit called her parents, who were birding in North Carolina. Larry was dazzled, hardly able to walk a straight line. When his best friend, Rocks, punched him in the shoulder and chuckled about the ball and chain, Larry grinned. "She makes me do hard time. Hard time."

He and Kit had been on their way to their engagement party when they had their first fight, a squabble about Larry's driving. Kit claimed he always hit the turns too hard and Larry, stung, punched the accelerator to illustrate how he never lost control of the vehicle for an instant. Kit glared and gripped the seat, then remembered to tell him that Rocks had called earlier. "He bought the lottery ticket. He told me to tell you he feels lucky."

"Me, too," Larry leered, scooting around another corner and trying to rest his hand on her knee until she shoved him away.

"Not lucky enough," she said. "Why don't you just flush that money down the toilet? Or give it to me. I could bring home groceries."

"Two bucks, twice a week. What are you going to bring home on that?"

"More than you have," she shot back, and wouldn't talk for the rest of the drive.

At the party was a huge cake from Kit's store that had KIT + LARRY ringed in white icing. Larry stood nodding while Kit thanked her employees by name, and he felt a slow oppression gather in his throat as the well-wishers shook his hand. He smiled, said his thank-yous, and knew he was a cliché: the groom with cold feet. Chattering with her friends, Kit looked unfamiliar and not pleasant, and Larry reminded himself that everyone felt this detachment, which didn't seem far from horror. The question, he thought, was not whether he and Kit were right together. The question was how anyone made it to the altar at all. When Rocks called him to watch the lottery broadcast, Larry bolted as if he'd snapped his leash.

The lottery blonde had already pulled out the first number, which matched theirs, but anyone who played the lottery knew that the first two matches didn't mean anything. Larry ticked his eyes over the lottery blonde. "When do we get to win her?" he asked, the joke he always made. He was reassured when her second number matched the ticket Rocks was holding; it seemed a good omen. Not until she pulled the third matching number in a row did he sit up, alert, his breath uneven. Odds were crazily against three in a row. He glanced at Rocks, but he was staring at the screen, a stern, fixed look on his face, even when Larry nudged and reminded him they'd never gotten so far before.

The lottery blonde seemed to be moving quickly and slowly at once. She pulled up the fourth number— 48, to match their 48. "Rocks, what's the pot tonight?" Although he knew, of course, everybody knew. His voice wobbled like a teenager's.

"Twenty-six mill."

"Think you could find a way to spend your half?"

"Naw. I'll give it to charity." Neither of them laughed.

Larry reminded himself that she wouldn't pick their last number— 06; every odd in the world promised she wouldn't. But he couldn't help himself anymore and dropped to his hands and knees in front of the TV, softly babbling and pleading as if some human transaction were going on. He trembled, and tears stood in his eyes; when he looked up after rubbing them, he saw the blonde gently setting the card reading "06" next to the other cards. Larry felt oxygen rush out of his body.

Then air and gravity came roaring back and he sprang off the couch, bellowing. "Rich! Rich! I!" He was leaping across the room, banging into his giggling friends and then leaping away again, unable to stop crying out disconnected words— "Never! Now!"

He lost track of everyone else—Rocks, Kit. Thirteen million dollars! Doors he'd never even glimpsed were wide open, calling his name; he imagined a boundaryless, glittering ocean. He banged into the table that held the engagement cake, sloshing orange punch over the icing. "Look out, now," someone said, but Larry laughed, took a cup of punch, and splashed himself in the face. A hand pulled at his elbow. "Larry," Kit said. "For Pete's sake, get a grip. Don't do this."

"All systems go!" he said, wheeling to look at her. She looked ungainly, mean, her body full of juts and angles. She criticized his driving. Words flew out of his mouth like rockets. "The wedding's off," he said.

Rocks told him later that people stopped talking then, but Larry didn't remember. He recalled fingering off a corner of the cake, and then jumping up onto the coffee table to do the bump with Dana Evans. Sounds kept pushing up from his throat; he was roaring. When did Kit leave? Her purse was already gone when Rocks got Larry to sit down and watch the tape of the lottery drawing so Larry could see Rocks had recorded it the night before, then gone out to buy a ticket with the matching numbers. "It was a *joke,* you moron," Rocks said, his hand clamped around Larry's arm. "Nobody won that night. You weren't supposed to—Christ."

"Don't do this, Rocks."

Rocks pinched Larry on the wrist, twisting the skin hard.

"What are you going to do? What are you going to say to Kit?"

"Kit?" Larry never told Kit about this part, but his dread was that somehow she knew, anyway. "Kit?" As if her name were a foreign word. "Kit's gone."

"Don't you want her to come back?"

"No," he said.

He did, of course, as soon as he regained his senses. It took a year and a half to wheedle her back, while fortunes at the restaurant started to crack and dwindle, and he dipped into savings for new menu covers. Kit refused to speak to him on the phone for two months, and he woke up mornings imagining he heard sniper fire. "I was crazy," he pleaded when she finally talked to him. "I didn't know what I was saying. All kinds of stuff was coming out of my mouth."

"You were clear enough to me," Kit sniffed.

"Babe," he crooned. "Everybody has doubts. The best couples in the world have doubts. Didn't you have any doubts?"

"Not then."

"It was something I had to get out. I'm ready now."

"I already told my parents we decided this was wrong. What do I tell them now? That we redecided and it's right?"

"Yes," said Larry. "Tell them that."

She hung up on him, but when he counted to ten and called back, she picked up the phone, which was progress.

In the end they sped through a snowy February night to a justice of the peace in Bellville, forty miles away, whose radio played bluegrass while Kit cried and laughed and promised to take Larry for her husband. Larry moved to kiss her for the first time in a year and a half, rediscovering the moistness of her lips as he tried to part them with his tongue. She bit him, then laughed. "Come on, husband. Let's get on with things."

"She's a spitfire," the justice said while Larry gave him fifty bucks.

"You don't know the half of it," Larry said thickly. Kit wouldn't let him lay a hand on her for the drive home, but that night they clawed and yelled until neighbors on both sides were banging on the walls.

"Happy, darling?" Kit croaked when he brought her coffee in the morning.

"Close enough," he whispered.

Happy. They lobbed the word back and forth in the months that followed. Larry eavesdropped on Kit's assurances to her parents. He walked around his apartment, blinking at Kit's pictures on the wall next to his own. Happiness seemed to be a state of perpetual surprise; he was still jolted to find Kit's car in the driveway. He took to giving himself quiet little pep talks—only natural to be having a little trouble, having never known true happiness before. Watching her bustle in the door with groceries, he reminded himself: This was the joy he'd fought so hard to win.

Kit's parents wanted to be called DeAnne and Roger, an intimacy that stuck on Larry's tongue. Kit hadn't prepared him for the three-story home or the Mercedes in the driveway, and Larry, unnerved by his new in-laws' padded, wealthy cheeks, could hardly meet their eyes. They made birdcalls to each other through the bathroom door and then chuckled fondly. They laid out an amazing breakfast, too; Roger had to put the leaf in the table when DeAnne backed out of the kitchen with raisin snails. "Kit told us breakfast is your best meal," she said, picking up one of the three forks in front of her.

Larry blinked. This wasn't true at all. Kit scolded him regularly over his refusal to eat before noon. "That Kit just can't keep a secret. What else did she tell you?"

"Never let you get behind the wheel," Kit said, leaning over to goose him and brushing her foot against his burned shin.

"Not one accident. Never even a ticket," he protested, wincing, but Roger was already on his way back into the kitchen, asking Larry if he was an orange-juice man.

"I wish you wouldn't drag out old arguments in front of your parents," Larry murmured to Kit.

"Just teasing, Parnelli."

"Do they know that?" He was off balance in the face of her rowdy high spirits, and he wanted to know where her dread had gone. It seemed to have drained into him.

DeAnne settled across the table, her smile already in place. "So, you're a restaurateur. You must eat out every night."

Larry glanced at Kit, who wore a stark grin and nodded to urge him along. "Yes, ma'am," he said, feeling his way. "Your girl likes a varied menu."

"You try to please her," DeAnne said. "That's good. A marriage can survive anything if the partners work to please each other."

"She keeps me working," Larry said, trying for a joke.

"Is there any more bacon?" Kit asked, getting up just as Roger came through the swinging doors, a sizzling plate in each hand.

"I cooked the whole pound," he said to Larry. "I thought just this once you'd like to get enough."

"What a treat," said Larry, even more careful now, and angry with Kit. What was she telling them? After a single piece of toast he felt uncomfortable, ready to leave the table, but DeAnne was pouring more coffee while Roger distributed the bacon, piling half of it on Larry's plate. Larry watched the strips cool, both annoyed and relieved that no one seemed to notice he wasn't eating.

DeAnne was talking to Kit about their vacation to North Carolina, bringing Kit up to date on friends and old neighbors. "Fred Pindell's home again; he can't hold a job with two hands. His father's got a management position open, but he's afraid to tell Fred about it. He says it would be easier just to close the factory now and save Fred the trouble."

DeAnne cut her eyes to Larry. "Fred is Roger's cousin," she explained, and he nodded, keeping a pleasant expression. "The family's been making furniture for generations. They're worth quite a lot—although not as much as some, of course," DeAnne went on, twinkling.

"Fred Pindell," Kit exhaled. "Good Lord. He taught me how to play fruit roulette." She reached into the basket at the end of the table, pulled out an orange, and cut it down the middle, setting both halves cut sides down. "Now, everybody mark the outside where you think a seed is. If you come up right, you get a kiss."

"There's a gamble worth taking," Roger said loudly, cross-hatching the rind and passing it to DeAnne, who made a mark opposite his with her pink fingernail. Larry studied the orange when DeAnne slid it to him, probing to feel the rind's thickness, the amount of membrane inside.

"A sporting man," Roger said. "Checking out the odds."

Larry looked up, feeling his color rise. "Go on now," DeAnne said. "We all know you're going to win." Careless in his embarrassment, Larry jammed the sharp fruit knife into the orange, slicing right down the side so the blade came out with a seed quivering on the end of it.

"What did I tell you?" Roger said as Kit leaned over to peck Larry on the cheek. "The man knows how to play."

"He's a winner, all right," Kit said. "That's why I married him."

By the afternoon, Larry was shaking with strain. He and Roger had retreated to the porch after the uneasy breakfast; Roger picked up the newspaper and read the NASDAQ index aloud for fifteen minutes. Finally he looked over his glasses at Larry. "Where do you have investments, son?"

"There's a checking account at First Bank of Elite." Roger chuckled and pointedly waited until Larry went on: "Right now everything goes into the restaurant. But I'm sure I'll be investing one of these days."

"You can be too cautious, you know," Roger said, then ducked his head and went back to the paper.

Kit trailed her mother from room to room, chattering ninety to nothing, and the one moment Larry was able to catch her in the guest bedroom, she told him that she and her mother were going shopping—DeAnne was already backing out the car. "There's nothing that can't wait, bacon breath."

"That's one of the things I want to talk about."

"A *joke,* dear. What's wrong with you? They must be

wondering where my other husband is. The big joker I told them about."

"I'm wondering where my real wife is. The one who refuses to eat at a restaurant." He was talking to himself; Kit had trotted out of the room, and just before he heard the car door slam outside his window, DeAnne whooped with laughter. Then the house was unnervingly silent, waiting for Larry to make one wrong move. He picked up a red glass paperweight, aware that it was worth more than he would think.

Outside the bedroom door, Roger cleared his throat and Larry jumped. "Son? I'm working on a project out here. I could use some help."

"Sure," Larry said, hearing how surprise constricted his voice as he swung open the door and saw his father-in-law holding a hammer. "Happy to."

The project was down in the basement: a porch swing, a surprise for DeAnne. "I work on it when I can, but she never goes anywhere for long. I tell her I could have been president, but she keeps needing me to unload groceries. Well, you know how it is."

"You've made real progress," Larry said—a lie. Stacks of rough cedar boards lay next to the wall, and Roger looked at them with mistrust. Larry himself had only the vaguest ideas of how anything got built, and he looked around for saws and planers. "Are you following a plan?"

Roger flapped his hand. "For a porch swing? Here, help me pull up those big two-bys." Larry tried to keep his movements synchronized with the other man's, but it wasn't easy; whether he wanted to hoist the wood higher or change direction, Roger only grunted, and Larry started to sweat, his hands marking the wood. "Don't spend much time in the shop, do you?" Roger finally asked.

"There's not much space for woodworking in an apartment."

"I gather you won't be there much longer."

Larry frowned. "It's a nice apartment." The ballooning, airless feeling from breakfast was back, and he resisted the urge actually to rise on tiptoe.

Roger frowned back and let his end of the plank rest on the floor. "Have you changed your plans? I appreciate your impulse to save, but a house is a basic investment. I hate to think of Kit and you cooped up."

"We're fine," Larry said. "We're strong. We can see through the tough times." He was aware of how apologetic he sounded—the force of habit.

"Good Lord, boy, what do you want?" Roger put his hands on his hips. "I don't mean to tell you how to spend your money, but there's such a thing as too much caution."

Larry straightened. "Could you tell me just exactly what Kit has told you?"

"No need to look so alarmed. She told us you two've been banking the lottery money, trying to think about the wisest way to spend it. I don't mind telling you that DeAnne and I were relieved that you were both being so sensible. Money like that—we've seen it change people. Kit has, too. The truth is, at first I think she was afraid."

"She was right about that," Larry said, hanging on to the wall now for balance, his burned leg pinging.

"Money's a good thing. You'll see. It's normal to be afraid at first, but you'll look back at all this and laugh. Have a family! Go around the world! There's nothing to stop you."

"I don't know how to start," Larry said.

"Buy a house. Make Kit a swing. You'll see—it will take care of itself." Roger squeezed Larry's shoulder and stepped back awkwardly. "I always thought I'd be the one to take care of Kit. I thought that was my job. But here you—I guess I can move aside."

"She relies on you," Larry said. "More than you know."

Roger smiled self-consciously and retrieved a thin, bright saw from behind the boards. He directed Larry to the cut lines he'd already penciled in and said, "I'll hold her steady. You've got the brawn." Larry hadn't held a saw since high school wood shop, but he took the tool and started into the wood, pleased with the smooth lines he made and the dry, sweet cedar smell that rose up to his face. It was an unexpected pleasure. Just as he smiled, the saw coughed and snagged, ripping out a half-inch chunk of wood before slicing into Larry's thumb and taking off the top of it.

DeAnne and Kit, exhaling cigarette breath, didn't return home until early evening, when the men were already back from the emergency room. Larry was lying down with the shades pulled, woozy from painkiller and the scotch Roger poured when they got home. Roger couldn't do enough for him, even though he had to know the fault was Larry's own, and Larry was thinking—what the hell—about having him bring the bottle to the bedside.

He had sawed his thumb down to the knuckle: eight stitches. Now his thumb was wrapped in so much gauze it was the size of a small lightbulb, and in Larry's unfocused vision it seemed to give off light. He looked forward to Kit's reaction. While he and Roger had been waiting in the emergency room, Larry had worked on a speech for her, starting with the bacon business and ending with the money. *Any other whoppers I should know about?* was part of it, or maybe *Just how sorry do you think I am?* He should have written it down. But he wouldn't be doing any writing for a few weeks.

When Kit did come in he said, "Hi."

"Egads. A damaged husband. What happened?"

"A saw. Your father's making a porch swing, but he doesn't want your mother to know."

Kit smiled. "He's been working on that swing since I was a Girl Scout. The only one who thinks it's a surprise is Dad."

"You might try telling him."

"You must be joking. We've spent years not knowing about Dad's swing."

"He could move on to other projects. Bone up on the stock market," Larry said, holding up his thumb to feel it pulse. "He's all set to manage our portfolio."

Kit folded her arms and leaned back so that her shoulders were supported by the wall, her face in shadow. "We could use the help," she murmured.

"You want to invite him in and go over the accounts? How long were you planning to tell them we were keeping thirteen million dollars in savings?"

After a pause, he heard a sniffling hiccup. "You want me to tell them the truth? Should I start with our engagement party?"

"They expect tours and world cruises. They think you should be wearing a goddamned crown."

"They don't think I should still be wearing a nametag at the Thriftway."

Larry made his voice high and pleasant. "A good wife helps her husband through the hard times. A good wife pitches in."

"A good wife consoles her husband every night when he comes home," she said, matching him high for high, pleasant for pleasant, coming out of the shadow to sit beside him on the bed. With a soft motion, light as a wing, she stroked his thumb. "But then, a good husband provides."

"Don't have much patience, do you? Or maybe it's trust you don't have."

"Nobody could have more trust than me," she said. "Every day I believe in you all over again. I'm not the one who comes home crying."

"No—you're the one who tells your parents I eat breakfast and win the lottery."

"You could," she said. "I tell them where we're going. It's more trust than you've ever shown." Her hand bore down on him, harder now, so his thumb throbbed and seemed to Larry it might explode right through its bandages.

"If you think we're going to have millions, you haven't been paying attention," he said. For the first time it seemed strange to him that they never talked about goals. They were so happy; it was hard to get beyond that.

"I told my mother today, in the car, you're a man who gets what he wants. You don't ever stop trying. No one can know that better than me."

"What if I don't want to keep trying?" he whispered.

"Christ, Larry, this is no time to gamble." Not gently, she squeezed his thumb, and in the burst of white pain he felt one of the stitches give. "What have we been building?"

"Nothing," Larry said. He sat woozily up, swung his legs over the bed, and pulled his thumb away before she could squeeze it again and make him cry out. "I'm going downstairs. I'm going to have Roger take DeAnne to the basement so she can be measured for her swing."

"Meaning?"

"If Roger clears things up with her early, he can avoid nasty disappointments later."

"Is that what you're doing? Clearing up?"

Larry shook his head. The longing to hold her ripped through him like a gale; he looked at the floor and tried to steady himself. "Not me. I'm clearing out."

On their way home, after fifty silent miles, Larry stopped to pick up a hitchhiker, something he and Kit had never done. Kit's face was pinched shut, and she didn't move when Larry got out to help the man, who stumbled with his duffel bag. Once they were rolling again, the man said his name was Lloyd, and he was coming home from a party.

Larry introduced himself. Kit kept her head turned. "Must have been quite a party," Larry said. "If it was worth hitch-hiking to."

"It didn't start so far away," Lloyd said, squinting out his window as if to glimpse whatever Kit was staring down. "It just—moved on me."

Larry grinned tightly. "I've been to that party."

"Not this one, you weren't."

Over Kit's snort Larry said, "I like parties. You never know what will happen."

Lloyd leaned forward and tapped the back of Larry's seat. "At this party a fellow took apart a refrigerator in ten minutes. Nobody thought he could do it. He won two hundred bucks off us."

"That's a good one," Larry said.

Lloyd tapped the seat again. "Two donkeys got throwed in the water. Did you know they can swim? When they got to the shore, they kept clubbing their own ears to get the water out."

"That's rich," Larry said.

"I've been to lots of parties," Kit broke in. "I went to one where the guys and girls swapped underwear. I went to one in January where we set off fireworks in the snow. Neighbors called police to report UFOs."

"Haw," said Lloyd. "I'll remember that."

She said, "I've been to parties with Miss Elerette County. She brought her crown with her, and a ham."

"How about you?" Lloyd said, tapping Larry's seat.

"I went to one," he began, trying to think ahead, invent. "Somebody wanted to go sailing, but there wasn't any lake around. There was this little valley behind the house, so we ran a hose out there and tried to block off the ends of the yard with bags of cement a guy had." Silence eddied up around him; he was even boring himself. "I saw a guy win the lottery."

"How much did he win?" Lloyd asked. "I won twenty-five bucks one time."

"Thirteen million," Larry and Kit said together. She went on, "I've heard this story before."

"He bought a house," Larry said.

"And a Mercedes," Kit said. "Two."

"Nice cars," Lloyd nodded.

"People have been waiting for him to leave," Kit said. "Take his two Mercedeses and go away."

"I would," said Lloyd.

"Me, too," Larry said. "But he just sits around and doesn't go. What do you make of a man like that?"

"He don't deserve all that money. Some people just don't deserve their luck."

Kit spoke up. "Was this the party where you guys ran the chicken up the flagpole?" Lloyd guffawed.

"No," Larry said, looking at her happy, confiding face in surprise. "You can tell about that one next. This was before."

Lloyd said, "You two are just right for each other. I can see why you're married."

"Us?" said Kit. "We're not married."

"We haven't even met," Larry agreed.

HER
FATHER'S
HOUSE

Lou Packard had thought that after her father died she would finally get a little time to herself. She imagined gliding through warm, fragrant days with the dignity of a banker and the tranquillity of a nun. She imagined the soft noise of clocks. But when he died nothing stopped; Lou got up early to put together a guest list for the funeral. He had gone suddenly, two days shy of his seventy-fifth birthday, his liver shrunk and hard as a nut. An organist from the funeral home, an utter stranger, called twice to ask about music.

Lou hated the public rush and untidiness of it. People she'd never heard of sent flowers; you'd think he'd been a head of state. The boy at the newspaper kept asking about time of death, cause, survivors. "Only me," she said.

"Wife?"

"Daughter."

"Address?"

"I lived with him."

"Will your home be open to visitors after the interment?"

"No," she said, only slightly embarrassed at how bald she sounded. It was her house now, every stick and brick, and she meant to be clear about it. "I'm living here," Lou said.

They had fought about the house, Lou and her father. She tried to remind him about storm windows, the importance of painting every third year. In her study she kept magazines on home maintenance in one pile, notebooks filled with lists in another: *Weatherproofing. New porch (?).* Her father didn't notice the puckering windowsills, the shingles curled up like bacon; his eyes were never fixed further than his next drink. Whenever she mentioned the ominous tremble of the water heater, he would do priss-lipped imitations of her. Lou had to sneak and wheedle before she could so much as make his bed.

At first she consoled herself that he would weaken. The quarterly checks from their estate manager allowed him to buy scotch and vodka by the case, and she'd seen the old drunks around the downtown square, knew what to expect: the shambling steps, the smell on him like a thick film. But her father stayed fleshy and pink, and the nights he passed in the drunk tanks only seemed to invigorate him. "You meet people!" he told Lou when she drove him home. "You don't make friends like this anywhere else."

More than once she'd opened the door to find his friends leaning against the doorbell. "Grover said to come anytime." Then the loose grin, the gentle sway. Lou learned to close the door, not that it made any difference. Operating on some kind of drunk's radar, her father found them and brought them home again, forcing her to hurry up the stairs, away from the slack-lipped chivalry and gropes. One night, when her father and somebody named Marty had *Kiss Me Kate* on so loud the window screens were vibrating, Lou finally burst onto the landing and screamed, "Jesus! Why don't you just bang pots together!"

She had expected a moment's abashed silence, but the stereo didn't even flutter. Instead, heavy steps clattered to the kitchen, and then came the crashing of iron skillets. "Woo! Woo!" hooted her father.

That night she yanked down a suitcase from the top of her closet and dropped two blouses and a scarf into it, but in the morning she unpacked. She couldn't leave. Even during the years in Denver with Vincent she had dreamed of her father's house, the sun so bright off its front windows that she woke with stinging eyes. She never talked about the house to Vincent, but eventually he learned to jeer in a tone remarkably like her father's. "What's that sound? That soft, sweet voice? Could it be?—Yes! It's your childhood manse, calling you home again."

"And what's that I hear?" Lou shot back. "Why, it's poor little Vincent, jealous of a house."

The marriage lasted five years, but Lou could hardly remember Vincent now, not even the color of his shirts, and could hardly believe he'd talked her into leaving her father's house. She looked back on the marriage with the same embarrassment she felt looking at photos of her teenaged self—the full stretch of her sophomore year she had refused to wear socks. Her father never learned Vincent's name.

By the time she came back home, she was thirty-seven years old. A cab let her out and she stood with her suitcases for a moment, looking at the peaked roof, the heavy gray siding, the windows that had been blinding in her dreams. Her father stood at one of them with a highball and a cigarette, and she squinted up to wave. "What is it about you?" he called. "You look *dusty.*"

She tried to smile. "The wild West."

"Are you telling me you went wild?"

"Not wild enough. Can I come in?"

"I don't know." She waited for him to say something else. Slow, humid air flattened her hair against her face, and the suitcase handles slipped in her hands.

"Don't do this to me," she said.

"You've been gone for a long time. How was I to know you'd be back?"

"For God's sake, Dad. I've just come home. Where do you expect me to go?"

"Where do people usually go?" he asked in a mild tone, as if he were purely curious.

"Home. They go home," she said, and moved up the walk to the front door, which gave as soon as she leaned on it.

She took an involuntary step back; the entry smelled so bad the air seemed to clot in her lungs. No wonder he had tried to stall her, Lou thought, but then she looked up through the glare—he had every light in the place on—to see her father picking his way down the stairs, his left arm scratching the bannister in a straight cast that reached all the way to his shoulder. "What did you *do?*" she said.

He frowned at her and then said with exaggerated slowness, as if talking to a foreigner or an idiot, "I *broke* my *arm.* There was a scuffle."

"Aren't you a little old for bar fights?"

"Aren't you a little old to be coming back home?"

"It smells like you've been slaughtering sheep in here. This place is going to hell in a handbasket, if you don't mind me saying so."

On cue, her father's eyes filled. "They won't let me do anything. I'm supposed to sit in a chair for three months." He bit his lip. "It isn't my fault."

"All right, Dad, hush now," she said, setting down her suitcases to take his free elbow and guide him into the living room. "You could have hired someone to come in. Someone to keep things up for you."

"They'll take the napkins, and I won't be able to stop them."

"Hush, now. I'm home. I'll go make you a cup of coffee. Won't that be nice? Some coffee?"

"And cookies," he said, sinking into the stained armchair. "Your mother would have made gingersnaps." He sat with his head tipped back, staring at the ceiling as if contemplating heaven, and Lou was wary. This was a new game. No telling which way he'd jump.

"She didn't stick around long enough to teach me gingersnaps," Lou said.

"She was a saint."

"The saint of running away. The saint of leaving-in-the-lurch."

His eyes flipped open. "So what does that make you? The saint of never-leaves? The saint of the bad penny?"

"You want me to leave?" Lou asked evenly.

"You said you were going to bring me coffee."

His grin unnerved her so that Lou backed into the kitchen, finding the coffeepot jammed behind two big cans of asparagus, a crust of something reddish flaking around its handle. By the time she came back to the living room, her father had moved to the couch and was steadying a brandy bottle between his knees, working at the cork with his good hand. "Help me with this," he said. When she handed it back to him, he took a long pull, then sniffed and eyed the coffee without touching it. "So now you're a grass widow."

"Guess so."

"Some of the greatest gals I've ever known were grass widows."

"Before Mom left, or after?"

"Lucy Loose, soft as a goose. She was a grass widow three times over." He grinned into the stained sofa cushion. "She always brought her own bottle. Did you bring your own bottle?"

Lou paused a moment. He knew she didn't drink; their biggest battle had come the night he tried to hold her mouth open and pour a Tom Collins into it. "You take care of that. I'll take on the rest," she said, too tired to enter into the old fight, and watched her father smile foxily at the upholstery.

In the weeks following the funeral Lou got phone calls from Vincent and three friends she'd kept dimly in touch with since college, as well as seven different investment representatives who talked reassuringly about estate asset management. She cried and hung up on them. She hadn't been able to cry during her father's last week in the hospital. Even when he was clutching her hands and calling her Irene or George, she'd remained stiff and dry. But the phone calls unleashed her tears, embarrassed as she was to keep sniffling and hiccuping in front of perfect strangers.

It was mid-September, the time her gardening notebook indicated was ideal to set out spring bulbs and work bonemeal into the soil. She needed only to make a trip to the garden center; Lou still had the shopping list she'd started years before. But she couldn't move. Some mornings now she stood at the stove and dug her nails into her wrists from sheer blank grief, which took such peculiar forms.

She kept losing words. When her next-door neighbor called, armed with poppyseed cake and a sympathetic expression, Lou began sentences as if she were rolling downhill, unsure about where or how to stop.

"In the hospital, they didn't give him enough—He died. He needed—"

"Food, dear? Care?" The neighbor leaned forward. "He needed more care?"

"Air," Lou said. "I tried to tell them! He couldn't breathe!"

"He was very sick."

"He was sick all his life."

The neighbor sighed and shifted. "Sometimes death is a blessing." She leaned forward and took Lou's hands in hers. "What will you do with the house?"

"I live here."

"A big house. Valuable. It's a lot of work."

"I do work." That wasn't what she meant to say, but Lou couldn't lasso the right words. When Vincent had called a second time to tell her he missed her, she said, "A miss is as good as a block."

The neighbor left soon, assuring Lou that she would be there if Lou needed anything, not to hurry returning the plate. Lou stood at the porch murmuring "Doris," although she knew perfectly well the neighbor's name was Clarice.

No one else came to console her, and Lou was grateful. She set tiny goals for herself, chores that six months before she would have attacked with gusto, like telephoning the first roofer listed in the Yellow Pages, then wincing for two weeks while the house shuddered under the crew's hammers. Lou stood at the hall window watching old felt and shingles shower into the backyard. After the roofers left she drew a line through #1 on her list, then put the list in her dresser.

Her sleep was hot and unhappy, and she woke up panting, certain she had heard her father call her. She dreamed of the night she had to drive all the way to Louisville for him, sixty miles. "How did you ever get so far?" she asked fuzzily.

"Don't you know? I told them you'd know. I was sure." In the real police station he had looked at her and snickered, but in her dream he looked fuddled by the question.

Finally, on a night when she had awakened three times before midnight, Lou crept downstairs to her father's bottle cache behind the stereo: a quarter of a fifth of Jim Beam and half a bottle of Four Roses. She took both bottles into the kitchen, mixed half a tumbler of Four Roses with tap water, held her breath, and drank it down. Her mouth smarted and her ears buzzed, and she stood with one hand on the chair back, waiting for something to happen. When the phone rang, she jumped like a grasshopper.

"Lou? I can barely hear you." It was Vincent.

"It's the middle of the night."

"You afraid of waking somebody up?"

"Don't be a"—she paused, searching for the word—"an ass."

"I was just sitting here thinking. There you are, all alone in your big house. I thought, Why, Lou's an heiress! Inherited the family fortunes!"

"Vincent, have you been drinking?"

"Have you?"

"I'm grieving."

"That's just what I mean," he said. "No telling what you might take to, in your grief. I could help you."

"You gave me grief already."

"That's a good one." Lou remained silent, and Vincent said, "A new start."

"You're a dollar short."

"Well, sure. But I miss you, too. Look, is it somebody else?"

Lou could hear her father's voice as if he were standing next to her: *Green as grass with twice the weeds.* Vincent? Herself? She had never asked him what it meant. "Sure," she said, and dropped the receiver into its cradle.

She felt light-headed, but nothing she couldn't attribute to a month without sleep. What had she expected? That she, too, would start banging pots? She giggled. It seemed funny to her that after all this time she could just reach out and have a drink. She rinsed out her glass, trotted up the stairs, and the instant she climbed into bed fell into sleep as if spilled there.

Lou established rules for herself: No drinking until after supper. No more than two drinks, and no mixer—she could dimly remember her mother crying, "Rye and ginger!" and Lou refused to play her mother's part. She knew it was important that she establish limits, especially now, stumbling away from the lip of limitless grief.

In the evenings, over her first and second drinks, she was able to think about her father, imagine the conversations they could never have had in life. "All I needed to do was relax."

You needed a little help.

"I was wrong about so many things."

You're a strong-minded girl. I've always said so.

"All my life I thought you closed doors. But you opened doors."

Perfectly happy then, unable to stop smiling, Lou would go to bed with the smoky flavor of scotch still curling around the edge of her tongue, and she would sleep without dreaming or moving.

She didn't take her first morning drink until a storm blew in and split her father's oak tree down the middle. She stood shivering on the back porch, her fingers grazing her throat. Her father had loved that tree, bragging that it grew as God intended, never pruned or shaped. It shed right through the year and cast a shade so heavy that nothing but moss would grow under it, but to see it shattered came on her as a whole new cause for grief. She took a drink to see her through the phone calls.

Her next morning drink came with the tree surgeons, when the whine of their chainsaws set china rattling. After they left Lou stood at the window, the bottle cradled at her chest, and looked at the raw hole where the tree had stood.

I climbed that tree as a boy. Hell, I climbed that tree as a man.

"It breaks my heart."

Pretty talk. You could have saved it.

"How can you say that? It was split right through."

If you'd had someone out sooner, it never would have happened.

Lou slowly turned, her lip curling. "You wouldn't let me mow the lawn. Are you pretending now that you would have called in men with chainsaws?"

You always exaggerated everything.

"You never noticed anything."

I noticed that you couldn't manage to get out of the house.

"Not as easy to run off as Mom, eh?" she snapped. "Rye and ginger. Together you two must have been quite an act."

With you as the grand finale. Dusty and divorced.

"Oh, shut up," she said, shouldering her way back into the kitchen to get some ice.

But he didn't shut up. The sweet sympathy she'd been able to imagine had dissolved, and his voice carped and nagged and buzzed. He circled her like a cloud of mosquitoes, and when she awakened in the mornings with a swollen face and throbbing that ran from her toes to her hairline, she reached for vodka and quoted him: "A restorative."

Of course, it was on the morning that Lou misjudged how much restoring she required that her neighbor Clarice came back again, mincing across the grass as if she expected to stir up snakes there. Lou snarled. What did this woman expect? Lou was grieving. When she went to the back door, she was careful to keep a steadying hand on the counter.

"I just got these catalogs," Clarice simpered. "Such pretty slipcovers. I thought you might be interested. Something new for your living room."

"Furniture in slips? How embarrassing," Lou said, which was foolish, but better than what she'd meant to say, something along the lines of furniture filling up every space in the neighbor's busy, busy brain.

Clarice raised her eyebrows and edged into the kitchen next to Lou, rubbing her arms as if she were cold. Lou blinked. It was cold outside. When had it gotten cold?

"I like to think about house projects at this time of year," Clarice was saying. "What else is there, once you're braced for winter?"

"There's always the water heater," Lou ventured.

Clarice peered at her. "Are you all right? Do you feel dizzy?"

"It happens. Braced for winter's embrace. You?"

"You know," Clarice said carefully, "it's important to keep things up. Talk. Psychologists say this."

"I learned to talk. He said that's what women were good for. You should have heard some of the ones he brought home."

"The house always wanted a woman's touch," Clarice murmured.

"Don't you think it's touched?" Lou asked, surprised. "I do."

"This could be a lovely home. I'll leave the catalog for you to look at," Clarice said. "You might get ideas."

"Let's hope so," Lou said, nodding good-bye and giggling. She imagined telling her father that at last she was getting ideas.

Lou poured more vodka as a reward, but the liquor tasted metallic, and she coughed. Things occurred to her that she might have talked about with Clarice—had the woman thought about blue for her shutters, which Lou had noticed could use a touch-up? Her eyes welled, which annoyed her. "No reason I should be feeling lonely now," Lou said, folding herself into the big armchair in the living room. "You left me alone enough."

It took a moment for Lou to register the silence around her, how deep it was. "Yes sir, left me alone night and day. Taught me how to be lonely in my own house."

High wind whined across the shingles. "You just love this, don't you?" Lou said, but she was muttering, halfhearted. Even with a headful of vodka at ten in the morning she couldn't force her father to talk. "I was never able to make him do one thing in my life, and that's God's sweet truth," she said to the fireplace. She finished her drink, put her glass down in the exact center of the coffee table, and went back to the kitchen to dial Vincent's phone number, dully surprised that she didn't have to look it up.

"You were right," she said when he answered.

"Who is this?" Vincent said.

"Everything," she said, beginning to sniffle. "But you shouldn't have blamed me. I never meant to be a bad wife. Now I'm a grass widow. Do you still cut the grass on Tuesdays?"

"Widow? My God, Lou, I'm not dead yet."

"Didn't you know what you were getting in me?"

"Look—can I call you back?" Vincent mumbled. "I can't talk right now."

"You can kiss my sweet Lorraine," Lou said. "Kiss her for me." She could hear Vincent still whispering at her to wait as she put the phone down and then, after a moment's consideration, unplugged it. On her way out the door she found a scrap of white ribbon left over from one of the funeral bouquets and tied it jauntily in the hair above her eyebrow. She meant to get into Clarice's house, and knew she'd need some proof of good faith. "I appreciate your visits," she said to the mirror. "It helps so much to have someone to talk to."

But when she wound up her neighbor's path and rapped on the glass storm door, no one came, even though Lou dawdled and coughed and peered into the side window. This was Lou's first social excursion since the funeral, and she didn't want it to fail so soon. She calculated. Downtown had shops where women went to finger wallpaper, carpeting, drapes; Lou could picture Clarice frowning as she held two swatches to the light. By the time Lou got there, Clarice would be ready for lunch. Lou could recommend a tearoom she knew, where ladies often had wine with their meals.

Two blocks away from her house she was already shivering—no scarf, no gloves, her ribbon sodden and trailing in her eye—but she put her head down and stormed ahead. The difficulty came in finding Clarice. She wasn't at the upholstery shop or the draper's. She wasn't at the florist. Lou thought she spotted the woman's perky curls inside the stationery store, but they belonged to another matron, and Lou backed, apologizing, out the door. She was sniffling in the cold, and the tips of her fingers were numb, which wouldn't be happening if Clarice hadn't come over with her idiotic catalog, or if Lou's father hadn't died. If things with Vincent had worked out. If her damn mother had stayed home. Lou crossed the street and plunged into a hotel lounge where she took a corner booth and a cup of coffee with comfort in it. On her second cup she looked up just as a woman tapped her on the elbow.

"You eaten lunch yet?" Although she was large, the woman had a dim, almost dainty look; her hair was whiskery, and the orange cardigan she wore bagged down to her thighs. Lou shook her head.

"Neither have I," said the woman. "You want to buy me lunch?"

"Why would I want to do that?"

"Be nice. A little company on a cold day."

"I don't even know your name."

"Gloria. Come on. What else are you going to do?"

She had Lou there. "What the hell," Lou said, and moved over to give Gloria room. The woman sat close anyway, the edge of her cardigan flapping onto Lou's leg.

"You could freeze, just wandering around these streets," she said, signaling over Lou's shoulder to the waitress. "Winter's coming on. You have to take some precautions."

"I take precautions," Lou said. "You should see my house. It's braced for winter."

Gloria turned and winked at Lou with a smile that was wide and sweet. "Take a clue. Order something bracing."

"You never know what's coming," Lou nodded. "Have to brace yourself." She finished her coffee in one swallow. "I was looking for my neighbor. Her idea of precaution is a slipcover."

"Cover up your slips," said Gloria.

"She would. Me, I love them. Slipping's the best work I've ever done." Gloria nodded, scanning the dark lounge, so warm it was steamy. Lou chattered like a teenager. "I kept lists. I had a list of household products that was four pages long. Proud? You've never seen it."

She paused only long enough to have the waitress bring them a carafe of wine. Then Gloria leaned her shoulder against Lou's and grinned again. "I used to read five newspapers. I attended sales events. I bought two pounds of tripe on special." She beamed. "I knitted my kids socks they wouldn't wear."

When the carafe was empty they ordered another, before businessmen, rumpled and red in the face, began to crowd the tables around them and Lou and Gloria switched to manhattans. Lou caught the businessmen glancing; even full drunk she could see how they smirked at Gloria's orange sweater. She drained her glass and stood up, gripping the back of the banquette as she felt her weight shift. "I propose," she said, "that we retire to my—" And here she lost the word, somewhere between *abode* and *home* and *digs,* so she carefully started again. "We can have music."

But Gloria shook her head. "Honey, I'm snozzled. And it's cold outside."

"They won't let you stay here."

"Don't know why not," Gloria said dreamily. "Toasty." She smiled and let her eyes close, so she looked like a movie siren. Lou watched a man at the table by the wall gesture to the waitress, then point at her and Gloria.

"Please," Lou said.

Gloria's eyes snapped open and she put her hand up. Too late, Lou thought. Already the man was coming over, a fluttery grin on his lips.

"Haven't seen you ladies before," he said.

"Two more of the same," Gloria said.

From the living room came a long gargling sound; Lou didn't need to look to know that Gloria had rolled onto her back. "You never realized all that you had," Vincent crooned, still kneading.

"You don't listen. I realized down to the penny. Down to the nail. Down to the husband who got bored and the mother who ran off. Down to the drop. Guess your memory isn't as good as you think." She jerked away from him.

"I believe in new starts," he said.

"That's funny. I believe in history. And you're inmine."

"This is a choice you're making," he said, the whine high in his voice. "I'm offering you a chance. You'll be lonely."

Lou smiled. With great gentle care, she set the broken coffeepot in the sink, then assembled a tray with vodka, tumblers, and a bucket of ice to carry into the living room, where it would soon be needed. "Get out of my way."

"They'll only stay as long as that lasts," he said, nodding at the tray.

"They're my friends."

"Friends bring their own."

"Not in this house. This house provides. It is"—she paused for the precise phrase—"generous in spirit."

"You'll have every souse and wino for miles in here. They'll be your friends."

Lou glanced at Clarice's house. She still meant to suggest blue for those shutters. She could offer to paint them herself. Her father would have said, *Waste of taste. Make sure a man can say thank you before you give him a drink.* "Some people need training," she said.

"Not them," Vincent said. "They're pros."

"They have so much to teach me," Lou said, picked up the tray, and waltzed into the living room, where gratitude was so thick she could smell it.

Stars

Della didn't hear about the Newly Single meeting until she came home and found grocery bags full of wine and crackers still unpacked on the kitchen table. From the bathroom the shower was whining, and Della sighed and fished out a cracker. If Trish would just *tell* her about these things.

The group met every week at someone's house; the members talked about reentering the unmarried world, how suddenly vulnerable they felt, or, more often, how large their lives had become, how wide their possibilities. Trish, who had been renting Della's extra bedroom since her own divorce began, gave full reenactments the mornings after meetings, and Della hooted.

Now, hearing the shower go off, Della printed OLDLY SINGLE on a three-by-five card and taped it to her bedroom door. "Starting your own support group?" Trish asked when she stepped, still dripping, out of the foggy bathroom and saw the card.

"Just letting you know where I stand."

Trish grinned. "You should join us tonight as a tribe elder. We're having a topic meeting: New Vistas."

Della made a sour face. She hadn't yet mustered the fortitude to tell Trish what was really waiting for her: mixers at the community center with four women for every stammering, pock-faced man; a medicine cabinet stuffed with vitamin E and eye-wrinkle cream; friends who talked about women's solidarity but would cheerfully scissor off your hands for a date.

"I wrote a talk. 'Being single is an adventure,'" Trish said now, padding toward the kitchen. "'It's an invitation to embrace life after so many years of death.'"

"You weren't dead," Della said.

"Life with Walter? Close enough."

"Cancer," Della murmured.

"Seven years. Eight, counting the time we lived together. Why didn't somebody stop me?"

"Because trying to stop you is like trying to stop a locomotive."

Trish laughed. "Walter called me a battering ram. I called him my castle keep."

"That's Cancer," Della said. "Sign of stability. Values home and hearth."

"He valued them every day, right down to the penny. It was like being married to an investment portfolio."

The description didn't sound so bad to Della. "How's your job hunt going?" she asked.

"Companies aren't looking," Trish said, and shrugged. The alimony she received from Walter was shockingly meager, a fact that Della resented more than Trish did. "I'll ask the group tonight if anybody's heard about openings, but you may need to float my rent for a while."

"Better hope something comes along, or we'll both go under," said nervous Della, Capricorn, who kept an eye on every dollar.

The money was tight, tight, tight. Across the Bay Area real-estate values were toppling, and Della was forced to hold open houses for hot little stucco shoeboxes that she would have turned down two years before. She was making cold calls again, leaving her business card in mailboxes like a beginner.

She had never meant to find herself, at forty-two, still living commission to commission and renting out the extra bedroom, but fortunes kept reversing on her. Her brother back in Terre Haute had siphoned off the small inheritance from their parents, and she had totaled two cars; now she had to sell a hundred thousand a year merely to keep up with her insurance premiums. She double-checked the almanac every morning, hunting for the shift of planets that would let her fortunes finally shine.

Taking in Trish hadn't helped; money seemed to evaporate every time the woman came in the door. She wheedled Della to join her at first-run movies and afterward pulled her to bars that featured expensive, creamy drinks. Della, who had never become friendly with a roomer before, felt herself soften and blur; she gained five pounds and bought a blue velvet coat at Macy's that absorbed three months' worth of clothes allowance. "It makes you look like a movie star. It's exactly what you want," Trish said, which was true.

"That's not the point," Della said helplessly. Trish seemed to know nothing about margins, nothing about walls that gave way, water heaters that burst. Sometimes Della thought Trish hadn't learned a thing from her divorce. Trish was the sort of woman, Della thought, who would marry again and again, and when she thought of Trish marrying, her throat clamped shut.

So when Walter called in early March and told her he wanted to sell his house, she was cool to begin with, even though the efficient, accounting segment of her brain was already clicking away, calculating percentages, possible overage. "I've been reading the real-estate reports. You can't be too busy," he said.

"It's a seller's market," she allowed. "Any agent will tell you."

"This is unpleasant for me. I don't want to go around interviewing people. Can you sell my house?"

"Of course," Della said, insulted and cautioning herself: *Careful.* "We can work any way you want."

"Quickly," he said.

"Naturally."

"I've kept things up. Interior and exterior painted every year," he said.

"A selling point."

"The roof—" But he broke down then, and hearing the bewilderment in his weeping, Della felt her own tears rise up; for the first time she imagined a real man behind Trish's gleeful imitations.

"I'll make it as easy for you as I can," she promised. "I'll screen out the Looky-Lous. You don't even need to be home."

"Do what you need to do. I've got to get out of here."

Della nodded. "Sometimes memories make it too hard. Then it's easier to start fresh."

"One thing—I don't want Trish to know. Don't blast it around, don't put up a sign. I don't want her walking back in the door."

"I know how to keep a secret," Della said. "You get to live your own life now."

He cleared his throat; Della pictured him getting a grip. "Have you been through a divorce?"

She was tempted to say yes—all the nights she'd stayed up while Trish railed. "I understand loss," she said.

"Let's get started soon," Walter said, the relief plain in his voice.

Della made it to his neighborhood in under half an hour, and then drove past the house twice, even though Walter had given her his address. Without ever intending to, she had come to believe Trish's dramatic, shuddering descriptions. A prison, Trish called it, a box with no escape. Della happily thumped her steering wheel and found a description of her own: exquisite. Notched into a steep hillside, the house gazed down a rocky mile to the ocean, its view unobstructed by so much as a pine tree. Della got out of the car and craned to see around the property, joyously taking in the cantilevered deck and the seamless walls of glass that wrapped around the whole second story, so clean that light seemed to tumble out of them. "Gorgeous, one-of-a-kind home," she murmured. "Landscaped grounds." These exquisite too, wide beds of bright flowers hedged with roses, lavish as a catalog.

Della beat her fist against her leg for the loveliness of it. She rarely even got near properties like this. They were represented by agents with murmuring voices who drove Mercedeses. Now Della was having trouble catching her breath, the air around her sharp as a new dollar bill. No telling where this sale would lead her.

She turned back to look again at the house and saw Walter watching her from a downstairs window. Him, at least, she recognized from Trish's description—light hair that shot up in cowlicks, lips thin as if he were trying to swallow them. Della smiled and spread her hands to indicate that she admired the property, to indicate her pleasure. He spread his hands back at her, a gesture of giving up.

"I made a list," he said when she hurried up to the flagstone patio. "The refrigerator is new, and I had a heat pump installed."

"There's a form—" Della began, but stopped when Walter handed her a fat accordion file. "That's every receipt and repair history," he said, and Della tried to limit the grin she could feel spreading across her mouth.

"Not many people are so organized," she said.

"Trish hates this file. She dared me to lose something. She said, 'Forget. Make a mistake.' Of course, later she pointed out lots of mistakes."

"She's a different sort of person," Della said, paging through the receipts. "Any businessperson knows that organization is essential."

"Too bad you can't make her see it your way," he muttered. She laid her hand on his arm and said, "Mr. Darnoff? Shouldn't we go inside, while it's still light?"

"Walter," he said. "I'm not old yet."

Which was true, Della thought, following him, but hard to keep in mind. He paused at the door to wipe his feet and straighten his jacket, actions she could tell were as natural as breathing. How on earth had he and careless Trish ever managed?

Then, stepping into the house, she forgot all about Trish. "Custom," she murmured, brushing her fingers over linen-textured wall covering.

"I visited warehouses," Walter said. "I went to the docks when shipments came in. I thought I was getting my whole life just right."

Catching sight of a wine-red ottoman soaked in the afternoon's gold light, Della nodded. "That's right."

"Trish wouldn't even take a bedspread when she left."

"She's spilled coffee on the one she uses now. Twice."

Walter was silent a moment, and Della was afraid she'd overstepped. "We replaced things," he said.

Della believed it. Dining room to breakfast room to kitchen she could see no chips, no frayed corners or smudges; the carpets might have been laid the day before. "Walter," she said. "This home will sell in an hour. People will fight for it. Are you sure you're ready to leave?"

"I'll start again. What's the option?" He tipped his head and frowned at her. "Hard to imagine starting by myself, though."

"Believe me; you won't be by yourself for long."

"No?"

"No." Della knew her smile was dazzling, and she wished he would look up to see it. "Trust me. This is what you're hiring me to know."

— • —

She stopped in the office on her way home. Working from the lists of comparison properties, she began to calculate asking price, commission: a new car, a workman out to look at her nervous heater. Clothes! And no more hungry reliance on Trish's two hundred dollars; for the first time in her life, Della would be able to live alone. She felt as if new blood were pouring through her, and pulled out the almanac she kept lodged next to her comp books. The answer was right there in front of her—a conjunction of Mars and Jupiter, with Venus in the fifth house. Positive aspects for business and romance. Della could feel the starry doors above her opening and beckoning her in; she was so relieved she was near tears, and wondered, not for the first time, how other people could bear to walk without guidance, day after day.

She drove home slowly, letting the night air tangle her hair, and worried lightly about how she would keep this new development a secret from Trish. She needn't have fretted—when she pulled up to her house, she found every light blazing, and music, so loud the harmonies wobbled and bent, surrounding the house like a force field. Trish often put on Motown when she was happy, although not usually so the whole street could hear.

The front door was stuck; Della had to shove it open and wedge herself in, finding that Trish had rolled up the living room carpet into the entry hall and was sweatily dancing with a strange man. He held her tight at the waist and dipped her, letting Trish's head bobble. They didn't look up, even when Della slammed the door and tried to clear her throat over the music—"I Second That Emotion," one of Trish's favorites.

Della was sure this wasn't a Newly Single man; he didn't have the ravenous, terrified support-group look. What he had was the stringy build of a runner, and he moved with calculated detachment, occupying his body as if he'd rented it for the night. His smile showed half an inch of gumline. Della instinctively crossed her arms and hiked up her shoulders, and watching Trish—upright now—rest her chin on his shoulder, wondered what bar they'd been in to get Trish in such a state. "Hey," she called out when the song ended. "Studio 54."

Trish smiled up at her. "Do you realize there is no place in this town to dance? It's a crime. Should be."

"We took things into our own hands," the man said, winking at Della as the opening bars of "I Second That Emotion" started again; Della winced, wondering how many times they'd played it through already. "The neighbors—" she shouted.

"Don't worry," Trish shouted back, spinning. "I unplugged the phone." She staggered and the man caught her, while Della sidestepped over to the volume knob. She had the impression, as she turned down the music, that shingles were being jarred loose.

"Spoilsport," Trish said, still dancing. She flashed a cheerful face toward Della. The man looked at Della, too.

"I'm Pete," he said. "You must be Della."

"All day long," she said. "Nighttime, too."

"He works at the bank," Trish said. "He thinks he can get me a job there. I told him I hate money, and he said in that case he's sure he can get me a job."

"In my line of work you want to be careful," Pete said, sliding his arm around Trish's shoulders. "But I just have a feeling about you." Trish leaned over and licked the bottom of his chin. Della felt her stomach tilt. "You two certainly have become fast friends," she said, tugging on the armchair's slipcover to keep from looking at them.

"Some things are meant to be," Pete said. "Written in the stars, like Romeo and Juliet."

"You might want to try looking at how those two ended up. Anyway, take a look at Trish's accounts."

Trish, thank heaven, laughed. "I haven't ever balanced my checkbook. It drove Walter nuts. He said quality people could account for every penny. Jiminy Christmas, he was dull. I hope I never have to see quality again."

"Hey," Pete objected.

"Cheer up, Romeo. Dull don't dance, and I found me somebody to dance with today," Trish said, catching hold of his belt and letting herself rock back on her heels while she glanced at Della. "What did you find?"

"Work," Della said. "I'm onto something big. Keep it down out here, okay?"

"We're just on our way out," Pete said, pulling Trish upright and leading her to the door. "You can have the place to yourself."

Della felt as if she were watching a car wreck. And although she knew how stupid it was to try to stand in fate's way, she actually ran after them and pulled Trish's free hand. "When will you be back?" she cried.

"Now, now," Pete said, sliding his hand around Della's waist so that both women were pressed up against him. "Don't you trust me, Della?"

"Of course she doesn't, silly," Trish said. She leaned across Pete to kiss Della on the cheek. "After a week, send out the dogs."

Over the next week, Della hardly had time to think about Trish; Walter's house dropped her into a whole new dimension of work. She called investment bankers whose sleek voices lapped at words, and she spent hours on the phone with other agents; clients for this sort of property didn't show up at Sunday-afternoon open houses. The first couple Della scheduled walked through the house jotting down their objections on a legal pad: difficult-to-clean wall surfaces, and the windows, a maintenance nightmare. The second prospect wore a Walkman and put a Coke can right on a lacquer-finish end table; Della didn't even show her the full basement, such a rarity in California.

"I thought you said it would sell itself," Walter said at the end of the week, when they sat together in the breakfast area surrounded by projections charts and calculators.

"A quality home calls for a quality buyer."

"Somebody sees a place, likes it, puts down the money. How long does this have to take?"

"Are you always so impatient?" Della asked. She worked a giggle into her voice, a teasing flick like a girl's. It worked; he lifted one corner of his mouth.

"A legacy from my ex-wife, who thought water took too long to boil," he said.

"She still hasn't learned that waiting can just make things better," Della said. "Your home will have an offer before you know it. I have a good feeling."

"Try to sell a house and you get a damn fortune-teller," he muttered, but Della heard the reluctant warmth enter his voice as he stood. "You want some coffee?"

"That would be nice." She smiled up at him. On the weekend they planned to go to Tiburon and look at a number of properties on the water, homes that would allow him to make a new start. Walter called her to double-check prices, square footage, tax base. It had been almost five years since a man had contrived reasons to call Della; when she got out of bed in the mornings she sang.

After four days she ran into Trish downtown, at the Sandwich Xpress where Della had stopped in for a late lunch; a conference call with two relocation agencies had dragged on for close to an hour, and other agents were making ungentle jokes about tying up the phone lines. Now Della stood in line and was intending to order both roast beef and chicken salad when she heard a wolf whistle and turned to see Trish waving her over. The woman glowed as if she might throw off sparks. "You haven't been worried, have you?" she asked.

"I figured you were all right," Della said.

"I can't tell you how I feel. It's like climbing up out of a grave."

"You look very happy."

"Happy? He's—I've waited a long time to feel like this." Trish's mouth quivered and flexed. "You should go out to dinner with us. You'll like him. He believes in astrology, too."

"My," Della said.

"He's a Pisces. Fish. He says that's why he wiggles."

"I'm pretty busy these days," Della said. "Work is picking up."

"I'll be home before long," Trish said. "I'll need some clean clothes."

Della smiled and nodded and got back in line for the sandwiches she no longer wanted. She didn't need an almanac to foresee this one; anyone could predict the mood changes, the silent phone, the excrutiating slide into doubt and despair. Fretful, preoccupied, when she came back to the office and a message from Walter, she didn't even pick up the phone. He called a half-hour later, anyway. No surprise.

"Did you get my message?" he asked.

"I was just about to call."

"I got impatient," he said, and then in a burst, "We'll be late Saturday. We're sure to take all day. Why don't we plan on dinner?"

At that moment Della hated her heart for starting to racket around, and she tried to push the blood down from her cheeks. "That's a good idea," she said. "It's practical."

"I hope it's more than that," Walter said with an awkward laugh. As soon as she hung up, Belinda Rorty, who had the desk across from hers, looked at the expression on Della's face and said, "Tut, tut. The office phone is not for personal calls."

"He's a client," Della snarled. Belinda hooted, and Della added hopelessly, "He is," though no one was listening.

Trish was in her bedroom humming "Baby Love" and folding underwear when Della came home Saturday night. Hearing her, Della was grateful for Walter's gentlemanly ways; he had seen her to the door but wouldn't come in. "Thank you for a lovely day," he'd said. Della knew she would have to leave her phone free Monday at ten for his call.

Now she ambled down the hall to Trish's room. "Hi, stranger."

"Hi, yourself. I was starting to wonder if I should call the police." Trish grinned, underwear draping both knees.

"Client," Della said, and couldn't resist adding, "A good one."

"Better watch yourself. Pete says you're a damn fine-looking woman. He likes your coat. He wishes more women knew how to dress with a little class."

Della felt herself blushing, which she hadn't done all night, even when Walter shyly told her how pretty she looked in the table's candlelight. "Pisces are flatterers," she murmured.

"He's a ruthless flirt," Trish said, snapping underwear elastic at her. "He hits on the teenage girls at gas stations."

"What do you do?"

"Keep one hand on his arm and the other on the car keys."

Della laughed then too, and sat down to help Trish fold. "So is he really going to give you a job?"

"Start Monday," Trish said. "He sent me home to do my laundry. We're going up to the city later."

"He's sweeping you off your feet."

"He knows how to show a girl a good time. And I'm overdue."

Della knew she should keep her mouth shut, but she had her own share of giddiness bubbling up. "I wonder what Walter would think of him," she murmured, looking down at the stained bedspread.

"Walter would have a catfit. I'm tempted to bring Pete over to the house just to see the fireworks."

Della refolded a pair she had already finished, smoothing out the wrinkles. "Things are lively with you around."

"You know what one of the women said at Newly Single? She said she knew she'd make mistakes, but she just didn't want to make the same mistakes."

"You're safe," Della said. "Does Pete balance his checkbook?"

Trish laughed. "Pete brings me chocolates and we go out dancing and when he looks at me my elbows get all wobbly. Della, I'm not looking for the same husband I just left."

"Good thing. I don't think Pete is anybody's idea of a husband."

"You'd be surprised," Trish said, looking almost embarrassed for half a moment, before she leaned forward and patted Della's knee. "Tell me about your good client."

"We looked at waterfront properties," Della stammered, appalled, but then Pete drove up; the sound of his car reminded her of gravel spraying from under tires, even though her driveway was concrete. "Your prince is here."

"Can you let him in? I still have T-shirts to fold."

So Della opened her door again to Pete, who smiled down at her. She hadn't remembered him being so tall. "Trish is folding her laundry," she said. "Last door to the left."

"I can wait for her out here," he said, touching Della's wrist and walking into the living room. "It's a nice room. You must have put a lot of thought into it."

"This is how it looked when I moved in."

"That's not how Trish tells it. Of course, she's Sagittarius. Likes to make things dramatic." Della sat on the ottoman, and Pete sat down next to her, so close he breathed into the part in her hair. "You don't trust drama, do you? Taurus?"

"That's right," Della muttered, edging away, rolling her eyes. "The bull."

"Astrology is more complicated than people realize. It's more than just birthdays. I'll tell you something." Pete patted

Della's knee, then let his hand rest there. "The first thing I do when somebody comes in for a loan is run their chart. I got software—I never make a loan until I can see the ascendant, trines, all of it. And you know what?"

"You don't have one default," Della said, nodding.

"The best record in the branch," he said, making slow circles with his hand.

"But if you try to tell anybody how you did it, they look at you like you're a crackpot," Della said. She was surprised at her own bitterness; she'd thought she had come to terms with this years ago. "I lost a client once because she heard me mention planetary conjunctions. She went to my boss and asked him for someone 'mainstream.'"

"What an idiot," Pete said, shaking his head. "I hope she got a house with a leaky roof."

"Garage fell down her second year there. Now she thinks the whole firm is shysters and loonies. She wrote us a letter saying so."

Pete laughed, then curled around with an odd motion so he almost encircled her. Della stood up hard, and he said plaintively, "Della, what does it take?" He put his hand on the back of her leg as if to implore her, and as Della heard Trish coming down the hall, she backed up so that Trish wouldn't see. Trish smiled when she saw them and said, "I'm almost ready," while Della's thigh grew damp under Pete's hand. "I hope we can be friends," he said when Trish moved out the door with her clothes. "We could be good for each other. I have people applying for home loans every day." He let his fingers crawl higher, making Della's breath stutter and catch. "I'm going to be persistent. We understand each other."

"You don't understand a thing. I'm not even Taurus. January fourteenth."

"Capricorn. I can see that," he said.

Persistent? Once she got her breath back, Della wanted to laugh. Pete didn't know the half of it. Walter called her at exactly ten on Monday, when, she imagined, Pete was hunched at his desk, his eyes still unclear from the weekend. "I went down to the beach yesterday, just for a walk. I tried to imagine living right on the water. Seemed like a good idea," Walter said.

"I was in the office. I'm glad one of us was out in the sun."

"Everybody was out with a dog. Do you like dogs?" His voice was cozy and close, and Della, hating herself, felt the urge to pull at her collar, to get away, get air.

"I never had one."

"When I came home I had veal," he went on dreamily. "Yours looked so good at the restaurant."

"It was a little tough," she said lightly. "I was just now sorting through the messages on my desk. A software designer is transferring from Connecticut. Also a surgeon."

"Tell him not to get blood on my carpets. There used to be a surgeon down the street. People said when he moved out the house was a pigsty. But the garage was clean."

"He knew his priorities," Della said, and Walter chuckled more than the weak joke required. She could picture him happily twirling the telephone cord; imagining it made her start to shake her head. "Maybe by the end of the week we'll have an offer. Are you ready to start packing?"

"I thought you knew."

"Come again?"

"I wasn't ready before," he said. "Things have changed. I'm ready now."

After she said good-bye and hung up, because she was alone in the back office and could get away with it, and because she suddenly felt trapped inside her own skin, Della swept the phone off her desk for the pleasure of hearing it hit the floor. Trish would have appreciated the gesture. Pete, she supposed, too.

Leaning down, she dropped the receiver back in the cradle and let her eye rest on the chart she had discreetly taped on the side of her desk. New moon in Libra, aligned with Jupiter. The best aspect in years. "Shit," Della muttered, and pressed her forehead against the desk's smooth wood. Romance and life changes were open at last, a readiness that was determined the minute she came into the world. At her feet the phone rang, and Della nudged it with her toe until the receptionist took the call at the front.

"Del-la!" the receptionist sang out. "It's Wal-ter!"

"I'm not he-ere," Della sang back flatly.

"Come on, talk to him. I don't want to take his calls all day."

"This is a favor," Della yelled as she reached down for the phone.

"I almost forgot to tell you—a banker called," Walter said. "He saw the listing and said he might represent several appropriate clients."

"The more, the merrier. I'll be happy to call him."

"This could be our lucky week. If you ask me, it's time to move on to other and more enjoyable business."

"I don't know," she said incautiously. "I'm a woman who loves her work."

"There's more to enjoy, Della. Don't you think it's time to widen your scope?"

"No," she said, amazed at what was coming out of her mouth. "I think it's time to bear down."

Walter paused. "We'll talk," he said. "Do you want this banker?"

"Let me at him," she said, growling, trying to make a joke, saving herself from having to say anything more while Walter gave her Pete's name, phone and fax numbers, home and office.

"Does Trish have any idea you're setting up to do business with her ex?" Della asked when Pete phoned that evening. Her stocking feet up on the arm of the couch, she was eating peanuts and licking the salt off her fingertips.

"I'm not doing anything. A few phone calls. How many phone calls do you make in a day?"

"She won't stick around, you know. She won't stay if she finds out."

"So what are you planning to tell her? I notice you haven't exactly practiced full disclosure yourself lately."

"My fiduciary responsibility is to the seller," Della said. She was enjoying herself, sure of her ground.

"That's what I like about you, Della. You never lose track of the big picture."

"I've been around the block. If you lose the big picture, you lose." Pete laughed, and Della licked more salt off her fingers.

"Okay, Big Picture. My bank has two clients looking for investment-quality homes."

"Are these your clients?"

"They might be, if we do this right."

"So I'm supposed to drum up your business?" Della asked.

"You've already started," Pete said. "I'll pick you up at seven tomorrow night."

"This is like trying to get flypaper off my hands," Della said, going after the last peanut. "What if I say no?"

"I'll come anyway."

"Trish is my best friend. Remember Trish?"

"I don't forget Trish for a minute. I told you the night I met you: Trish and Pete were written in the stars."

"So where are Della and Pete written? In the small print?"

Pete laughed again. "You're tough, Della. I like a tough woman. And there are lots of stars."

Della had expected to be nervous the next day, but in fact she felt buoyant, easy; she knew she was sparkling, and made a point of phoning several old clients while she was in such good form. She talked to Trish, too, who called to suggest she and Della meet for dinner, a suggestion Della rushed past. "Let me guess," Trish said twice. "The sun has moved into Jupiter?"

Della refused to be baited. "Why, the sun's in Pisces now. I would have expected you to know that."

"I should have," Trish said grimly, and Della heard the fear in her voice. "Is it time to move my things out?"

"Not yet," Della said.

She talked with Walter, too; he had spent the morning packing boxes of inessentials, and was planning on a movie for that night. "Go. Enjoy yourself," she said. "I won't be in until late."

"All work and no play."

"I have a plan. If I work late now, I can keep the weekend free." Walter pretended to grumble, but Della heard the relief in his voice, and knew he had planned another Saturday night, but didn't mean to ask her before Thursday. Della planned to say yes, and to sound happy about it, too.

Pete, to her surprise, arrived at her door a few minutes early. They stood on either side of the threshold and grinned at each other. "Come in," she said.

He shook his head. "If I come in, I won't be able to keep my hands off you."

"Then let's go," she said, excitement running through her so quick and light that her hands shook as she closed the door behind them; she was frantic, wild as a teenager to be touched. "You know this is a very bad idea," she said as he started the car.

"I don't know that at all." He turned to her and rested his finger in the hollow of her throat. "So, where are we going?" he asked.

Della directed him to Walter's house, to let Pete see for him-self the custom window treatments. To increase the drama, she made Pete stay in the car when they got there, and hurried in-side to hit the floodlights Walter had positioned under each of the olive trees. She swung the heavy front door wide and called, "Allee, allee, all come free."

"Are we playing a game?" he said when he came to the door.

"Of course," she said, unable to stop laughing, knowing he would kiss her before she could so much as close the door. They didn't even get to the dining room before they were on their knees, making noises from high in their throats, and Della, thinking of Walter's pride in his thick carpet, dug her fingers harder into Pete's arms.

When they finished Della rolled away from Pete and listened to the stillness around them—an owl outside, and the wind through eucalyptus leaves making a sound like silk. Wealth, she realized, bought this plush quiet. She'd never thought of it before. From here she could probably hear the sound of the planets. Turning her head away from Pete, she listened to the air, taking it in like sweet water. Distant gulls. The light wind. And then the sound of a car.

"Get up." She pulled on Pete's arm; he was logy, half asleep. "Get *up!*" She was already shoving her bare feet into shoes, tucking panty hose into her purse, shaking her hair to make it uniformly wild; she could blame it on an open car window. She checked the carpet, but it didn't show a mark, and she blessed Walter again for always buying quality.

As she heard Walter's footsteps coming in from the garage, Della yanked Pete hard into the far corridor, where she flipped the lights first on, then off. ". . . So you can see the advantages of the floor plan," she said loudly.

"Della?" She heard the dread in Walter's voice and she marched Pete into the kitchen, talking fast, as hard as she could, introducing Pete, the banker Walter himself had sent her. Walter's eyes skated over the two of them, and he licked his lips several times.

"I'm sorry we didn't warn you, Walter. We were in a late meeting, and I knew you were planning to be out."

Pete said, "I might have a buyer. Della here was explaining

that you want to move quickly." He rested his hand on her shoulder, and she shuddered it off.

"Very," Walter said. Della watched his eyes flick away from her, and, panicking, she laid her hand on his arm and walked him into the laundry room, leaving Pete to inspect cupboards.

"I'm so glad you came in," she murmured. "This guy is an octopus. I've been sidestepping him all night."

"I gathered," Walter said, looking at Della's lips, which she knew were frowzy and swollen.

"We can see him out; he brought his own car. You can bring me home later. Walter?" She squeezed his arm as he half turned from her and she took a shaky, chastised breath. Her eyes flooded then, and her voice cracked. "Walter, *please*."

Finally he turned back and met her eyes; his were dry. "He's cheap," Walter said. "I'm surprised you had anything to do with him."

Della pressed her lips against the responses that needled up in her. Had Walter ever taken a breath he hadn't thought about three times first? Did he ever get tired of his tiny, impeccable life? Just looking at him made Della long to get stupid drunk.

"I want him out of here," Walter finally said. He walked back into the kitchen, turning off the light as he went, an infuriating bit of chintziness. Della thought of the new moon, the starry doors open above her. Doors, she thought, could also be closed. She smoothed her hands on her skirt and found that her blouse was rucked up at the back, showing half an inch of skin. She ran her finger across the spot. "The hell with it."

When she came back in the kitchen, both men turned toward her, and Pete reached out his cupped hand. "I guess I'd better take you home," he said.

"No need," she said, and smiled.

"No," Walter agreed, his voice tight.

"The night is young," Della said. "There's still time for a little business." Still smiling, trembling, she crossed the kitchen to the telephone and dialed from memory, counting hand-painted tiles to keep from looking at the men. Her breath was so unsteady she was practically hiccuping by the time she was able to say, "Hi, Trish. I was hoping I'd catch you." Loudly, so both men could hear.

LIES
OF
THE SAINTS

MARY
GRACE
(1958)

From upstairs, Mary Grace heard laughing. Kevin was up there with his tutor, and the two of them were supposed to be going over French, which Kevin was on his way to failing for the second time. He seemed deaf to the cognates, indifferent to the grammar's nice symmetry; Mary Grace couldn't understand his difficulties. "It's like a puzzle," she tried to encourage her son. "It's a game."

"That's pathetic," he said.

So Russ had brought home this woman who worked in the buyers' office at his furniture company and had a degree in French—Marsha, with tumbling red hair and feet tiny as a child's. Whenever Russ came in the room her head shot up and she blinked and smiled, the pulse vibrating in her throat. Mary Grace teased Russ about Marsha's adoring eyes two or three times a week.

Now, though, Mary Grace stood at the bottom of the stairs and listened to the muffled giggling. Kevin had pulled a C- on his last exam, and his teacher had written *Not out of the*

woods yet across the bottom, where Kevin had made a snarl of
the progressive past tense. "Hey, you two," she called. "I want
to hear some learning going on. I want to hear suffering."

She heard a chair slide back, and then a terrific thump—all
of Kevin's bulk hitting the floor. "I'm suffering! I may die!"

"That's more like it," Mary Grace said. "Keep it up."

"Knowledge is pain? You're sure that's the lesson you want
him to learn?" Russ said from the kitchen table. Ignoring his
doctor's advice, he was having a late-afternoon cup of coffee.

"A lesson, any lesson. We can work out the fine tuning.
You're going to pay for that coffee later."

"Got to have a few pleasures in life."

"Some pleasures don't make your stomach hurt."

"Don't you believe it. Sooner or later they all get to you."
She rolled her eyes for his benefit but didn't move from the
foot of the stairs, straining to hear quiet murmurs of explana-
tion, the reciting of vocabulary. Instead, Kevin's nickering
squeal erupted again, and Marsha's titter.

"Call me a skeptic," she said.

"Come on, Madame Crack-the-Whip. They don't have to
stay on it every second."

She turned unhappily to look at him. "Yes, they do. They're
in a room by themselves. Please, Russ—say something.
They'll listen to you."

"They're just laughing. You have a very rigid imagination,"
he said, shaking his head and draining his cup before he stood
up.

Not true, she thought. Her imagination was lithe and flex-
ible and made her wish Russ would pick up a little speed on
the stairs. What came next was predictable: She heard his mild

knock and some few words, not even enough to remind them of Kevin's next exam. Marsha said something, and then Kevin, and then the laughter of the three of them unfurled like a banner down the stairs to run out at Mary Grace's feet.

The day kept going downhill. At dinner Patrick accidentally shot ketchup right across the table, onto Mary Grace, the windowsill, and the café curtains, and Paul needled James until the younger boy howled and Russ had to step in. Tracy, the baby, started to fuss before the meal was over; Kevin pushed back his chair and muttered, *"L'enfant crie encore"*—the baby is crying again—the one French sentence he had memorized correctly. After the dishes were cleared Mary Grace walked the baby and brooded.

Just a year earlier Kevin had been an easygoing child, smart and sardonic and his father's favorite, though Russ tried to pretend otherwise. But Tracy's arrival—a surprise, God knew, to them all—had tipped Kevin into snarling adolescence. While the other boys rallied, setting up a betting pool for the birth date and squabbling over names, Kevin stayed in his room and read *Superman*. He wouldn't look at his mother; when she invited him to come feel the baby kick, he thumped her belly as if it were a watermelon and said, "Hi, Bud."

"You could try a little respect."

"For what? The miracle of life? Gee, Mom, you sure seem miraculous."

"Why do you have to be so ugly?" she said, rubbing her stinging eyes.

"Why do you expect me to be so happy all the time? You're the wonderful font of life. You be happy." He punched a pillow on the arm of the couch and ran out of the room before he had to see her cry. Russ sighed and went after him.

The memory still made Mary Grace's eyes cloud, even now, while she squinted into the mirror to pluck her eyebrows with her free hand. She knew Kevin was helpless, at the mercy of marauding hormones, but she was a thirty-nine-year-old mother and cursed with a few hormones of her own. She'd already told Russ that no other woman in the obstetrician's waiting room had gray hair.

When Russ finally came upstairs and reached around her for the milk of magnesia, holding a fist against his abdomen, she fluffed the grayest hanks over the collar of her robe. "I'm thinking about going red."

"Now? Just when you're starting to look distinguished?"

"Kevin, our charming son, used the word *grizzled*. How's your stomach?"

Russ swigged a mouthful of medicine, easily twice his dose, straight from the bottle. After he swallowed he said, "Grand. I'm taking this for the pleasure."

"I'm going to start hiding the coffee."

"In that case, go ahead and shoot me now."

"Nice try," Mary Grace said, "but you're not leaving me alone with all these kids. How's Kevin doing with his dialogues?"

"He can't keep the words in his head for two minutes."

"Maybe he needs a less distracting tutor."

"If he had half the crush on her you think he does, he'd know his irregular verbs backwards."

"Okay, Solomon," Mary Grace said, watching the way Russ ground his fist into his abdomen. She wished she could massage it for him, but he wouldn't let her touch him when he hurt like this. "Then what's the problem?"

"Patrick broke in on Kevin and Marsha three times this afternoon. No wonder the boy can't concentrate."

"That won't happen again," she said grimly.

"The record player. The baby. Everybody slamming in and out six hundred times a day."

"Family, Russ. It goes with the territory." Mary Grace heard the sharp note in her own voice and stopped talking; this was no time to start sniping. She straightened the blanket around the murmuring baby and listened to Russ bang the vanity with his ankle, an aggravating sound.

"Marsha thinks it would be a good idea to take Kevin places with her—the grocery store, the beach. She thinks he'll concentrate better if they get out." Russ paused, then banged the vanity harder, as if he were one of the boys, trying on pain for the pure sensation. "It's a fresh approach."

"It's fresh, all right," she said. "Kevin hasn't gone to a grocery store with me in a year and a half. But I suppose the produce section has new appeal if Marsha's there to weigh grapes for him." The baby whimpered, and Mary Grace murmured *shu-shu-shu,* trying to derail the angry cries she could feel approaching.

"Lord, what a mind you've got," said Russ. "She's not going to seduce him. What do you think she is?"

"Young. Unmarried. Lovesick over the boy's father. I hate to think of the vocabulary she might feel moved to teach him."

"She wants to start with the beach, while it's still warm enough. I'll go as a chaperone and keep an ear on them. Will that make you happy?" Something thudded into a downstairs wall so hard the closet door rattled, and Russ leaned into the hall to yell, "Can you please keep it *down!*" At his cry Tracy pushed away from Mary Grace and screamed, Russ looked over his shoulder and spread his hands, and against her will, Mary Grace agreed with him. Who could study through this commotion? Herself, she could barely breathe.

"All right," she said, bouncing the baby and making chukking noises. "But I'll chaperone with you; I'll take Tracy. She ought to provide plenty of vocabulary." Mary Grace smiled at Russ's rumpled expression. "Think of it as a family outing with a friend."

"You haven't been thinking of her as a friend up to this point. You haven't spent five minutes talking to her."

"High time I started," Mary Grace said, and, pleased with her solution, she hurried the wailing baby downstairs so Russ could get some peace.

As it turned out, Patrick and James wanted to go to the beach, too, even though the day was gray and clammy and Mary Grace made them wear sweatshirts against the blowing sand. She smiled apologetically when they met Marsha. "I didn't mean for this to be such a group event," Mary Grace said.

Marsha was wearing a pale yellow jacket that made her hair seem to pulse with color. Watching Russ and the two young boys fan out across the sand, lobbing a football one of them had brought, she shrugged and said, "They'll give us something to talk about." Nodding at Kevin, she pointed down the beach. *"Le football est brun."* Mary Grace could imagine it in a textbook: *The football is brown.*

"Oui," Kevin agreed. He pointed at a seagull. "What's that?"

Marsha wrinkled her nose. "*Il est sale.*" Dirty, Mary Grace recalled, surprised at the reach of her memory. "Stinks, too," she murmured, meaning only to talk to the baby, who was waving her hands happily, but Marsha nodded. "*Puant,*" Marsha said, holding her nose.

Kevin laughed and pointed at Patrick, waggling the ball over his head and high-stepping at the surf line. "*Puant.*"

"Very funny," Mary Grace said.

"*Mais oui!*" Marsha said, going on that he'd made a joke, *une blague,* very good. Kevin grinned and pointed at the green lifeguard station—*vert*—and an old red bucket lying in the sand—*rouge.* They were baby words, first-week vocabulary, but Marsha nodded and encouraged him, *trés bon, c'est ça.* Then the boy pointed right at Marsha and said, "*Rouge,*" a blush rising to his own face as soon as the word was out; he turned and stared wretchedly at the low, lisping surf.

"*Oui,*" Marsha said gravely. "*Rouge brillant.*" Mary Grace, relieved on Kevin's behalf, translated for him: "Bright red."

"I knew that," he said, then jumped to his feet; the football had scudded over James's hands and was bobbing in the dirty shallows. Kevin thundered out, splashing water to his waist, and shot the ball back to Russ before Patrick could get to it. Russ caught the pass neatly, tucked the ball and started to run; Mary Grace laughed, wondering who he was imitating.

"He's quite an athlete," Marsha said.

"Be sure to tell him that. He probably won't be able to walk tomorrow."

"He says he plays with the boys all the time."

"It isn't always so strenuous," Mary Grace said, watching Marsha watch Russ, who was bent over, laughing and panting. "These days he tells the boys to respect his twilight years."

"He isn't old!" Marsha sounded angry, and Mary Grace said, "Try telling that to a fifteen-year-old." She watched Russ whoop and leap for the ball. Only after dinner would the muscles in his calves and lower back start to ache, and the pain would make him walk around the house and point out every smudged wall and nick in the furniture veneer.

"Even on bad days he can make you see the bright side," Marsha said. "The secretaries all love him."

"He pays," Mary Grace said. "Some nights when his ulcer's bad he can't even stand up."

Marsha looked sharply at Mary Grace and frowned. "Is this a joke? He never told me about an ulcer."

"That's Russ. Looks on the bright side."

"But he drinks coffee all day," Marsha said. "I've seen him order spicy foods. He drinks Cokes. Scotch!"

"He's not an ideal patient."

"I'm surprised, that's all." But she was blinking, and her voice rode unsteadily up and down. Mary Grace couldn't keep herself from feeling sorry for the woman. "How could you have known?" she said, the same tone she used to soothe the kids. "Anyway, it's just a small hole. The doctor says it isn't much. That drives Russ nuts."

"Of course it does. He's in pain."

Mary Grace was about to say, "He'll live," which she and Russ and the boys said to one another all the time, but the shocked look on Marsha's face stopped her. "He knows how to live with it," she said.

"Is that supposed to be comfort?" Marsha said.

"It's not bad comfort, once you get used to it." Mary Grace reached out to block Tracy from crawling off the blanket onto the cold sand. Kevin ran back up the beach to them, hit the blanket next to Marsha knees first, and sprayed sand all over her legs. "Dad says he has an arm like a cannon," Kevin said. "I said, right, more like a water pistol."

"*En français,*" Marsha reproved him.

"I don't know how to say that in French."

"*Exactement,*" she said.

The next exam was another C-. "I don't understand it," Russ said, sitting at the kitchen table with a glass of milk. "He felt confident. He told me things were starting to make sense."

"Guess he's not the best judge of that," Mary Grace said. She was washing lettuce for dinner, trying to tamp down her own disappointment; her mouth seemed to have ashes in it.

"I think he gets nervous."

"Thank you, Marsha."

Russ shot an annoyed look at her. "You have a better theory?"

"Sure. The test might ask more of him than Marsha does. 'The football is brown.' She doesn't believe in challenge, does she?"

"Marsha," Russ said, "can tell when a test is coming up just from the tension in his shoulders. She volunteered to talk to his teacher."

"Does she think his teacher hasn't noticed that Kevin's still barely passing? What *does* that girl see?"

"You want to tell me what you're talking about?"

Mary Grace smacked the lettuce into the sink and turned to face Russ. "She practically cried when she found out about your ulcer. I asked her if she goes out on the weekends and she said she's usually too tired. Sometimes she stays down there at the showroom twelve or thirteen hours. My God, I said, you must be there all by yourself. 'I like to just walk around,' she said. 'I go into the offices upstairs and think about what goes on there.'"

"She's a hard worker." He smiled. Mary Grace found the sight repulsive.

"Russ, this is not your finest hour."

"You ask a lot. Not one thing has gone on between us. Not one thing ever will."

"You think of her. You bring her home." She held on to the sink to steady herself.

"I introduce her to my family. For crying out loud, Mary Grace, if I was planning to run off with her, do you think I'd show her my kids?"

"You want it both ways. You want that poor girl walking through the showroom because you walked there."

Russ's hand hovered over his ribcage. "Believe me, having Marsha walk through the showroom isn't what I want."

"Jesus Christ, Russ!" she cried, suddenly afraid. Whatever he was going to say, she needed to stop him.

"You want to hear it? I'm a hero."

"You think I don't know that?" she said, taking a kitchen towel and twisting it around her hand until her fingers started to tingle.

"I am doing my best," Russ muttered and stood up. "My level best."

He turned and went upstairs. Mary Grace stayed where she was, her hands clamped on the ledge around the sink, until she felt the wave of dread recede. By that time Russ was back in the kitchen, walking wordlessly to the door that led to the garage. "When will you be back?" she asked.

"I'm going to the office."

"Kevin wants you to go over his homework."

"Tell Kevin he can call Marsha. He's got her number." Russ slammed the door, a gesture he must have been saving for six months. Tracy woke up howling.

Her throat thick as a fist, Mary Grace walked the baby and tried to sing, but Tracy thrashed and pitched, and the boys, one at a time, closed their bedroom doors upstairs. Bitterly, Mary Grace thought of Russ sitting in a dark office, the air around him quiet as cotton. She was so distracted that a half-hour passed before she looked at the mottled flush over Tracy's cheeks and thought to take the baby's temperature: 101.

"I'm so sorry, sweetheart," Mary Grace said as she nudged a dropper of baby aspirin into Tracy's mouth. She rocked the tiny, hot body as it tried to curl away from her. "Nobody listens, do they? Nobody hears a word you say." She stroked Tracy's angry cheeks and realized hopelessly that everything red now reminded her of Marsha. *"Rouge,"* she whispered.

Well past midnight Tracy finally eased back to sleep, her fist falling away from her mother's chest. Mary Grace laid her in the crib and watched her murmur and reach; she'd been born so full of wants. "Better get used to that," Mary Grace whispered to the crib, then kissed the air above Tracy's head and felt her way downstairs.

After setting a bottle in a saucepan with an inch of water, Mary Grace closed her eyes and gently rested her forehead against the cool refrigerator. The house's deep silence trembled around her. Had Russ been home they would have felt obliged to talk; so much, every day, got crowded out. Mary Grace, eyes still closed, calmly hoped that if Marsha was working late tonight, talking was what she and Russ were doing. Tracy's bottle chattered in the boiling water. "Do you want me to turn this off for you?" She jerked up; Kevin was standing beside the stove, his face very white.

"I couldn't sleep," he said.

"Sorry," she said. "You need your sleep."

"I'll live." He shuffled and poked the saucepan handle. "How's Tracy?"

"She'll be fine."

"Sure put on a show. Bet you started thinking again about parenting as a career option."

He wasn't wearing a robe over his pajamas, so she could see his dense, tense neck. Mary Grace wondered what test he had coming up. "You were no stranger to tantrums. You made us put in our nights."

"You've told me."

"The winter you were three, you didn't sleep. I don't think you dozed off once. I kept calling the doctor, begging for tranquilizers. Your father fell asleep in meetings."

"I've heard this."

But now that she was started, Mary Grace was ready to talk. "We had snow that winter. We broke records. Every plumber for miles was booked up, dealing with frozen toilets. I couldn't get the house warm, so I made you and Paul wear three sweaters. Every time I turned around you were taking yours off."

Kevin wandered to the doorway. Keeping his back to Mary Grace, he slouched and fiddled with the latch. "Loose," he said.

"Of course you got sick, but it was a night with snow and I was afraid to get in the car. After your fever went over a hundred and four, I couldn't make myself check it anymore. We kept calling the doctor, who told us to put you in a tub full of ice water. I emptied ice trays, your father brought in a pailful of snow he'd scraped up, and we tried to lay you down. You thrashed and kicked; you were throwing ice all over the bathroom, bellowing. Poor Paul was terrified outside the door. And you were so hot! The snow melted the second it touched you."

"That's what snow does, Mom. It melts."

"So finally your father took his clothes off. You could see your breath in that bathroom, and he took you in his arms and laid down in that freezing tub with you, holding you next to him until you quieted down."

Kevin toyed with the latch some more. "So what's the point?"

Mary Grace shrugged. "Darned if I know. We haven't had snow since."

"*Neige*. It snows around here once every twenty years. Why do I remember that word?"

"All the wrong stuff sticks," Mary Grace said. She turned to take Tracy's bottle off the heat, and Kevin ducked back up the dark stairs before she could tell him to.

Russ came home an hour later, when Mary Grace was singing to the baby in the living room. He held out his arms and Mary

Grace handed her to him, their actions fluid, harmonious. In the morning they got the boys off to school and Russ out the door without having to exchange a word.

Mary Grace took a quick shower while the baby slept, soundly for once, and then leaned toward the mirror to brush on rouge and blot lipstick, measures she hadn't bothered with in six months. Greasepaint, Russ called it. Mary Grace imitated a clown's expression of startled delight for the mirror, and added a third coat.

She paused downstairs to collect a sweater and hat for the baby, and saw that Russ had cleared the breakfast dishes, swept the floor. She nodded. He was dotting every *i,* putting himself above reproach. She appreciated his punctiliousness, and told the baby so on the drive over to the showroom. Then, once she had listed all of Russ's attributes, Mary Grace started to sing. She was on the fifth verse of the froggy who would a-wooing go when she parked in a visitor's space, gathered up Tracy, and edged into the front office. The receptionist glanced up blankly. "I'm Russ Neill's wife," Mary Grace said.

"He's in a meeting."

"That's fine; I'm here to see Marsha."

The receptionist smiled at Mary Grace then, full of pointed interest. "Is she expecting you?"

"We're friends," Mary Grace said. It wasn't a pure lie, she argued with herself as the receptionist got on the P.A. Then she heard Marsha's quick footsteps and looked up to see her quick, tiny hands gesturing Mary Grace out of the reception area, over toward bunk beds. "Kevin called last night," Marsha murmured before Mary Grace had even sat down. "He was very upset about the test."

"I had no idea. He didn't say anything to us," Mary Grace said. "What did he tell you?"

"I can't—he asked me not to tell. But you need to understand; he's right on the edge."

"He's fifteen years old. Life at fifteen is one long edge." Mary Grace smiled and rested a kind hand on Marsha's arm, which stiffened. "His father says Kevin could get the golden goose and complain about having to clean out the nest."

"He's not happy!" Marsha burst out.

"He's never been the kind of kid who goes around spreading sunshine." Mary Grace sat on the edge of one of the bottom bunks, putting Tracy down to squirm beside her. "I tell him he's his father's boy."

"You're wrong. Russ is the happiest man I know."

"He rises to occasions," Mary Grace said, nodding. "But keep your eye on him. He turned to me once at a swim meet of Paul's and said, 'You think this adds up? Christ, I'd give my whole life away for just one thing I could hold on to.' I kept the kids away from him then."

Marsha stared at the carpet under her shoes. When she looked up again, her eyes were wet and webbed with red veins. "Why would he say such a thing?"

"He's an idealist," Mary Grace said softly. She hated this memory, too, and always tried to put it aside.

"That's true!" Marsha cried. "He's full of dreams; dreams keep people from going under. He's the one that told me that."

Mary Grace sighed; she'd heard the speech, too, more than once. "I see it differently," she said. "Dreams remind him of what he hasn't got. Just when he's in danger of being content, a dream comes along."

"Other people would call this ambition. I always thought it was a virtue."

"Maybe he's virtuous enough." Mary Grace frowned at herself; none of this was going the way she'd meant. "I'm trying to be happy," she said.

"And you're asking me to help?" Marsha laughed sourly, watching Mary Grace fence the baby off from the edge of the bed. "The first time I ever walked into Russ's office I saw the picture of all of you. Paul, Kevin, Patrick, James, Tracy. He rattled them off and I memorized them, right there. It seemed so *good*."

"It's what we got handed," murmured Mary Grace.

"Here was the whole package, everything hanging together. I wanted to warm my hands over that picture."

"What did you think you were seeing?" Mary Grace cried, half outraged and half ready to laugh. "Patrick flushed James's hamster down the toilet last week. We don't sit around at night and sing."

"You keep each other going."

"No, we don't. We hold each other in place. Although I didn't know that until you came along to point it out. It's quite a shock to find out that you're miserable."

Marsha looked across the showroom floor. Mary Grace saw the knuckles of the hand clutching the bunk rail whiten. "I'm sorry," Marsha muttered, the hand clenching and releasing. "I can't tell you how sorry. Is that what you came to hear me say?"

"For Pete's sake. I came to take you to lunch."

The slim spine jerked straight. "You really are," Marsha said, "just like Russ." She walked away fast, her shoulders actually shaking under the force of her anger. Mary Grace, embarrassed, pulled Tracy onto her lap and started fussing with her diaper. She shook her head at the salesman who started to move toward her from dinettes. "I don't need any help," she called to him, louder than she'd meant.

In four days Marsha was due to pick up Kevin for a trip to the post office. Mary Grace suffered the wait impatiently; she intended to apologize and see if they couldn't start afresh. Memories kept swimming back to her—Russ's childhood fears of glass and of chickens, his mother's fear of rain. She was back in possession of details she hadn't recalled in twenty years, since her blushing-bride days, and she wanted to share the memories with someone.

She wouldn't be sharing them with Russ. He and Mary Grace had hardly spoken since their quarrel; she didn't even know whether he'd heard about her trip to the showroom. They dressed and undressed silently, and at night they slept hard on either side of the bed. Mary Grace tried, but she couldn't help feeling relieved. "Fine," she whispered while she brushed her teeth, knowing he was waiting outside the bathroom. "Good. Wait."

She wasn't thrown off her stride until Marsha called, the day before she was supposed to meet Kevin. Without even saying hello, she began, "I need to change the plans. Kevin can wait until next week."

"He won't think so," Mary Grace said, clutching the receiver with a hand that trembled a little.

"He doesn't have another test until the end of the month.

Anyway, he's stopped calling me since I pointed out that he always has plenty to say. Like his *père.*"

"With you, maybe," Mary Grace said. "Around here we've taken vows of silence."

"Everybody keeping his dreams to himself? Enjoy it while it lasts," Marsha said and hung up before Mary Grace could tell her about Russ making up songs when the boys were babies, singing the stock index or the names of every Democrat on city council.

"Marsha, right?" Russ said as she gently put down the receiver. He and Kevin were eating sandwiches at the table.

"Well. Garbo speaks."

"Garbo yourself. Session's off?"

"She says whatever he has to say, it isn't in French." She looked at Kevin, annoyed at his silence. "Well?"

He shrugged. "I don't have anything to say."

"Pretend," she said. "It will do you good."

"Did she say why she can't make it?" Russ asked. His voice was carefully even.

Mary Grace shook her head and Kevin cried, "Ha!" Then, catching his mother's look, he intoned "Ha!" again, through his nose, as if laughing in French. Russ laughed, too, after glancing at Mary Grace.

"What do you two find so hilarious?" Mary Grace said, folding a kitchen towel so it hung straight.

"There's an upholstery supplier in town," Russ said.

"From Marseilles." Kevin kissed the tips of his fingers. "He is weak in the face of great beauty." Russ chuckled and coughed, which Kevin took as encouragement. *"Que tu es belle, ma chère,*" he whispered throatily, surprising Mary Grace, who hadn't thought he could have put the sentence together.

"Stop it!" she said. She rammed her hands into her pockets. "What's the matter with you?"

"What's the matter with *you?*" Russ asked. "It's just a joke."

"It's ugly. It's no way to talk about her."

"What do you want, reverence? She can't hear us."

"So you can say anything? What do you say about me when I'm not around?"

"None of the same things," he said flatly. "You don't have to worry."

Mary Grace, feeling her lips quivering, crossed the room to the sink and splashed cold water on her face until the threat of tears was gone. When she turned around again, drying her face with a pot holder, Russ and Kevin were watching her with identical crafty expressions that she longed to wipe away. "When your father and I were first married, we used to dance at parties," she said.

"What are you talking about?" Kevin said.

"Thank God those days are over," Russ said at the same time.

"I, unlike your father, was a good dancer," Mary Grace said. "He never wanted to dance, but I missed it. Sometimes I'd say yes when other men asked me. There was nothing wrong with a turn in somebody's living room."

"Mary Grace," Russ said. "Where are you going with this?"

"A neighbor of ours gave a Christmas party one year. He had taught dance before the war; he dipped all his partners, even me, four months along with Paul." She glanced at Russ, who was shaking his head and staring at the table.

"He made me feel light—that's important to a woman. We did a spin but his foot caught on the rug and the two of us fell right onto the couch."

"He was smack on you. No telling what harm you could have done to the baby."

"Your father got up and turned off the music. Then he pulled me up so hard he ripped my new red dress at the shoulder." Kevin, avoiding her eyes, sidled over to the refrigerator, which he started to tap with two fingers.

"Tell him what happened before that, while you were still on the couch," Russ said. "Don't leave your story half-told, Mother."

Mary Grace hadn't thought of this party for ten years, and was shocked that the old memory could still make her light-headed. "There was mistletoe hung up all over the ceiling. He gave me a kiss."

"We all waited for you to come up for air," Russ said, his voice raw. "You didn't look like anybody's wife, I'll tell you that."

"I wasn't. It took years to learn to be a wife."

"Am I supposed to thank you now that you're all finished?"

"I just wonder if you're glad. Now that I'm all finished."

Russ took his time to answer, and Mary Grace flinched, even though his voice, when it came, was gentle. "You keep me in place."

"Your ball and chain?"

"That's not what I said."

Mary Grace dropped her eyes first. Kevin began to pound his fist softly against the refrigerator, making a hollow boom. "Stop," she said, but he didn't. "I don't know why you guys keep talking," he said. "I don't understand a word you're saying."

SAINT
TRACY
(1968)

Russ was doing his best to hurry home, but traffic had seized up, and as he listened uneasily to the station wagon's lugging idle, he imagined Mary Grace flashing around the kitchen, muttering every time she glanced at the clock. Let *her* waste half an hour while the idiot from production talked about vinyl analysis. Russ had shot out of the office, hoping to pick up a birthday card and rosary for Tracy on the way home. But now he was caught in this congealed traffic, helplessly watching the faint February light drain away. Angry headlights flicked on, pair by pair.

He bounced his thumb on the bottom of the steering wheel. *For God's sake, Russ.* Mary Grace said it often, managing to sound as though she were asking a favor on God's behalf, an inflection Tracy had picked up lately. "For God's *sake,*" Russ said now, craning around to see if he could squeeze into the outside lane. Just as he turned to look, the station wagon's engine died.

Instantly the driver behind Russ leaned on the horn, and then two or three others joined in, rattling him. He tried to turn on his hazard blinkers but the whole system was out, and when a truck air horn howled, Russ wrenched the door open and screamed, "What do you think, I just nodded off here?"

His hand was shaking so hard he tripped the key out of the ignition; it fell behind the brake pedal and he had to snake his arm down and grope. When he came up with it his hair caught on the St. Christopher medal Tracy had insisted on dangling from the visor. "Jesus H. Christ on a *crutch*," he yelled, yanking the medal free and throwing it against the back window. The bottleneck had abruptly opened and cars zipped past on both sides, drivers mouthing at him and shooting the bird. It took Russ three more tries to get the engine to spit back to life, and then he drove with two feet, goosing the accelerator even when he was stopped. By the time he got to the church, where he was supposed to pick up this rosary that Tracy wanted so much, all the windows were dark. Then Russ's foot slipped on the accelerator and the engine guttered out for the last time as he flooded it.

He tried to sneak in through the laundry room when the tow truck dropped him home, but Mary Grace ambushed him at the door, Tracy half a step behind her. "Well! Look who's here," Mary Grace announced while Tracy said, "Hi, Daddy." Two months ago, before she read a book about St. Thérèse and entered this saintly phase, she would have raced out and wrapped herself around him like a vine.

"Hi, sweetheart. Happy birthday."

She let Russ kiss her cheek, then walked sedately back through the kitchen while Mary Grace was yelling to Patrick and James to come to the table; they were finally going to eat. She looked up at Russ. "Did you get the you-know-what?"

He shook his head and kept his voice low. "Church was already closed when I got there. Ask me about the car."

"I hope you got her something, anyway."

"The car crapped out on the way home. It's at Whitie's now. They had to give me a lift."

He saw her glance into the dining room, where Tracy was already seated with her head bowed. "The child was counting on this. You might have tried calling."

He cleared his throat, feeling his mouth tighten. "Let me explain it to you again. The car collapsed in rush hour on the San Diego Freeway. Not a lot of phones out there, Mary Grace."

"Sorry," she said, and headed for the sink, picking up a head of lettuce.

"I'll explain it to her," he said.

"Darn right you will."

Russ stalked out of the kitchen, so angry he could barely walk; nothing in him wanted to bend. Fishing a piece of paper from his briefcase, he sat on the arm of the sofa and drew a rough rosary that wound up looking like a caterpillar dragging a cross. "WE O U 1 ROSARY," he wrote, and signed it "Love, Dad." Mary Grace could do what she wanted.

He could hear her laughing from the kitchen, bringing the casserole to the table, making James pour the milk, checking Patrick's hands. When Russ stood in the doorway to watch, Tracy's face was serene. She was floating well above the tension, adopting her mother's aggravating air of sanctity. Russ had devoted much of his married life to reminding Mary Grace that she was made of the same mortal flesh as the rest of them; he was damned if he was going to start the same battle with his daughter.

Meanwhile, James and Patrick were crying, "Birthday girl!" and pulling out their package, the wrapping paper wadded and bunched over one end. "How nice," Tracy murmured after unwrapping the glossy statuette of a girl in prayer; Russ had to admit that it wore the same woozy, rapturous expression as Tracy when she talked about God. "It's called 'The Little Flower at Prayer,'" Patrick added, glancing at Russ defensively.

"Good choice, son."

"It's beautiful," Tracy said, her voice high with emotion. She set it next to her plate before she reached for Russ's note. She looked happy, expectant, suddenly a child again, and Russ's stomach dropped. He couldn't believe he'd given her an IOU. He should have brought her a puppy; she loved puppies. "Oh," Tracy said, and he winced. "It's a promise. Thank you." Her face was shining, and she slipped out of her chair to kiss Russ on the cheek, and then Mary Grace. "I've been praying for this," she said. "Will it come soon?"

"Depends on your father," said Mary Grace.

"Like lightning," said Russ, his voice weak with relief. "You won't know what hit you."

Once Russ brought her the rosary, Tracy wouldn't let it out of her sight—she slept with it wrapped around her wrist. That Friday night, as she and her mother were making lemon bars, Tracy sifted powdered sugar with the beads knotted around her apron ties. The crucifix at the end, as big as Tracy's hand, banged into her calf when she walked, and so far Russ had managed not to say anything about it, but he didn't know how long he could hold out. He leaned in the doorway, complaining.

"We should never have bought that car. In the shop every week. It's starting to burn oil, too."

"It has a nice ride," Mary Grace said.

"That nice ride has run us six hundred bucks this year. I told you I didn't trust Fords, but you wanted those maroon seats."

"Calm down, Russ. Things happen to all cars." She poured flour into the bowl without bothering to look at him. "I don't know why you're taking this so personally."

"I keep track. Somebody has to." Russ held out his hand and started ticking off items. "There's the mortgage. The kids' tuition. Next month is auto insurance, for the three weeks a year the car actually runs. Then property tax. You aren't paying attention."

Mary Grace shrugged. "The money always comes in somehow."

"Not if Whitie gets there first," Russ muttered. He didn't want to say any more with Tracy in the room.

Tracy turned on the mixer, setting its shrill engine on high. "You know, Dad," she shouted over the whirring beaters, "you're not being very forgiving."

Russ counted to ten, staring at his daughter who stood blinking at him, and then said, "Who are you so sure ought to be forgiven here, Miss Scales of Justice?"

"Mom. She was only trying to help." She cut the mixer off and added, "You got mad all of a sudden. Anger never helps anything."

"Look—just make your cookies, Tracy. This isn't your business." He could tell by looking at Mary Grace's shoulders that she was holding back laughter, and it only made him angrier. He hoped she'd burn the damn lemon bars. "Your mother isn't all that practical."

Mary Grace glanced over her shoulder. "What do you want me to say? That you don't bring home enough money? Russ, if you don't want to have a little faith, what do you suggest?" She sniffed, and for a second Russ thought she might cry, but she turned toward the oven, putting out her hand for Tracy's pot holder. Russ backed out of the way.

"If you would just open your eyes for a second, you'd see that the world isn't what you think," he said.

"I'll remember that, Solomon."

Russ couldn't make a joke or go put his hand on Mary Grace's shoulder, though he knew things would go better if he did. Instead, Tracy came up to him and rested her head against his chest in a posture that had to be uncomfortable. "I pray for you, Daddy," she said.

"That's fine," he said. "I'm sure I need it." Tracy nodded solemnly while Mary Grace snorted from the sink, and Russ left the kitchen for his recliner, where he could read for a while without anyone praying over him.

In the morning he and Mary Grace rolled out of bed without speaking—not quite fighting yet, but trembling, on the lip. Russ heard Mary Grace and Tracy reciting prayers in the girl's room while he was shaving, and he bore down so hard he scored out a box of skin next to his mouth.

"I'm going out," he announced in the hallway after he bandaged his face.

"You said you were going to paint the shutters this week-end," Mary Grace called through the door.

"Weekend's a long time. You just keep your mind on higher things."

"Every time I look up I see shutters that need painting," Mary Grace said. On his way out the door Russ entertained himself with the vision of Tracy urging her mother back to her knees, apologizing to heaven for her unruly temper.

Russ patted the checkbook in his pocket; he knew just where he was going. The idea had come to him in the night, an inspiration so simple and elegant that it felt like wisdom. Now he whistled all the way to the strip mall, where he usually only went for stopgap coffee and bread. At the far end, just as he'd remembered, was a Pet Palace.

When Russ entered the store, which smelled of urine and sawdust and manufactured pine scent, he hesitated only a second. Behind the cash register was a girl with a spectacular pimple high on her cheek. "Can I help you?" she said.

"Not yet." In cages all the way at the back were the puppies; they started yapping and trying to stuff their heads through the bars as soon as they saw him. A fuzzy white one on the bottom row ran in tight circles, screeching and spraying urine in a six-inch arc.

"Special today," the girl said. "Thirty percent off the dogs on the bottom."

"Are they stale?" Russ asked.

She shrugged. "They've been here awhile."

Russ surveyed the dogs, some so big they could hardly turn around in their cages. He was glad Tracy wasn't here to see them. The salesgirl was intoning next to him about shots, vet checks, pedigrees. "What's that one?" Russ pointed to the only dog who wasn't barking, curled up in a tight brown-and-white ball with its back to them in the bottom corner.

"Basset," she said. "Ideal for children. We accept personal checks and all major credit cards."

"Those are the sad ones, right?" Russ asked, enchanted. Tracy would love a suffering dog.

"You'll want some puppy chow too. Also a leash."

By the time Russ got out of the store, he faced a half-mile walk uphill with two heavy bags and a puppy who didn't want to be held; its long body kept slithering out of Russ's arms, and twice it dived for the puppy chow. Russ kept his good humor by envisioning Tracy's face, and she didn't let him down: When he walked into the kitchen and let the puppy skate across the linoleum, she burst out, "He's for me, I know he is! He's my surprise!" She ran to Russ and covered his chin with kisses, then dropped to the floor in time to watch her puppy trip over its own ears in its eagerness to get to her. Russ was richly pleased with himself.

"This is a surprise," said Mary Grace from the door.

"I thought it was time to do something for my girl."

"There are those who might say we already have."

"I wanted to get her a real present," Russ said, watching Tracy roll on the floor and squeal as the puppy tugged at her shoelace. "This one's from me."

Now the fat was in the fire, all right. Mary Grace spat out pieces of argument from bed or the shower. "I can't believe you would just do this. Without even talking to me."

"I can't believe you would deny your daughter something that makes her so happy."

"This isn't about Tracy. It's about trust."

"Nope," said Russ, enjoying himself. "It's about Tracy." She rushed up to him as soon as he came home, detailing what the puppy had done and what she meant to teach it. She hugged Russ seven times a night. Even finding out that the car's alternator was shot couldn't tamp his glee. "So we'll fix it," he said.

"How much will it cost?" Mary Grace asked.

"Does it matter?"

"I guess not. There's apparently money for dogs. But what if Whitie says a thousand dollars?"

"The money always comes in somehow," he said sunnily. He was operating out of strength; he had gotten an end-of-quarter bonus, money he hadn't planned on, and he hadn't told Mary Grace yet.

She glared at him now and called Tracy, reminding her they'd have to leave soon for the weekly prayer service. "Tracy?" she called.

The girl came in, blushing and clutching her puppy. "I don't think I'd better go tonight," she said. "I don't think it's a good idea to leave him alone too much."

"You can leave him with your father. He'll make sure nothing happens."

"He's my dog. I have a responsibility now." Tracy brightened. "But you can pray for us."

"Good idea," Russ said. "Pray for quick housebreaking."

Mary Grace's mouth quivered; he could see she wanted to laugh despite herself. "I'll pray for you," she said. "I can't think of anybody who needs help more."

"Being a sore loser is unattractive, Mary Grace. You just wish you'd thought of a puppy first."

"Dog food," said Mary Grace. "Kennels. New carpeting. You're not being all that practical."

After the front door closed Tracy said, "I'm going to call him Francis."

"I always thought Sparky was a nice name."

"Francis," Tracy said, grinning as the puppy hauled itself onto the sofa, where it wasn't allowed. "St. Francis. He made friends with a wolf, you know."

"I'll bring home a wolf next. We can name it after your mother," Russ said, and was rewarded with his daughter's chiming laugh.

He was surprised at how little he knew about dogs. Tracy ran to him with questions: Was the puppy old enough to teach tricks? Would he choke on a Monopoly house? Russ walked back to the Pet Palace to get a book on puppy care. "Make your commands crisper, Trace," he said that night. "He needs to understand what you want."

Mary Grace lifted one eyebrow and said, "Russ! Come sit down for dinner."

"Very funny."

"It doesn't seem to work," she said, and when Tracy started to giggle, Russ woofed and trotted into the dining room, swinging his head from side to side and sniffing.

"Sit," Mary Grace said.

Russ showed his teeth. "Don't push it."

After dinner he closed the door to his study and read more, nodding at vaccination schedules and making his way through the dreary chapter on canine diseases, most of which seemed to attack nursing bitches. The information seemed irrelevent to Francis, who was a merry dog despite his grieved expression. Already he had learned, to Russ's delight, to wait at the door for Tracy; every time she came home he tried to fling himself into her arms. The cheerful uproar was like having a baby in the house again, and Russ wondered why he'd waited so long to get a dog.

By the time Russ paid off Whitie in cash and drove the car home again, Francis was starting to get the hang of housebreaking and Russ caught Mary Grace feeding him scraps in the kitchen. "Just fat," she said. "I'd have thrown it away. It's good for his coat."

"Been reading up?" he said.

"I've raised all the other babies in this house," she said, dangling a bit of meat in front of him.

"Guess a puppy wasn't such a bad idea."

"I'm biding my time." She tossed another scrap to Francis, who missed it and barked when it skidded under the oven. "Don't get cocky."

He was cocky, though, he knew it. After Tracy went to bed the puppy sometimes plodded in to see him, collapsing with his head on Russ's foot. Russ wouldn't move, waiting for Mary Grace to come by and get a gander.

One such night, when he was reading the paper for the second time because Mary Grace refused to walk past, Russ noticed that the puppy's breathing was louder than usual. He leaned over to pet him and soothe away whatever dream Francis was having, then jerked his hand away; the pup's chest was heaving and hot. Alarmed, Russ noticed how dull the eyes were, the nose dry as a biscuit. All of the diseases he'd read about bled together in his memory and the puppy laid his head back down, panting harder. Russ called for Mary Grace to come, to hurry.

She was the one who found an all-night emergency clinic, she the one who drove while Russ, trembling himself, held the shivering, panting animal wrapped in an old baby blanket. "Keep that dog away from the others," the receptionist snapped when they came in, even though Russ wouldn't let him out of his arms. "Don't you know what can happen?" Francis was giving off a rank smell, and when Russ tipped the dog's head up, he looked at Russ without recognition. The receptionist brought them into an examination room next, even before the German shepherd with a gunshot wound.

The veterinarian only had to glance at them. "Distemper. Christ. If you're going to get a dog, why aren't you willing to take care of him?"

"They told me he was vet checked," Russ mumbled, but the man had turned his big back to assemble syringes. "We'll take some blood and give him Keflex, but I don't know why I bother. He'd have had a chance if you'd brought him in before."

"We didn't know," Russ mumbled, furious at how pathetic he sounded.

"Listless? Sleeping a lot? Appetite off?"

Mary Grace said, "He always sleeps a lot. He's a baby."

"Jesus. Do you have kids? I hope you take care of your kids better." He plunged the first needle into the puppy's hip and glanced at the chart. "Francis. Jesus."

"We can keep him quiet and warm, Doctor," said Mary Grace. "Just tell us what to feed him."

"What do you think distemper is? This dog isn't going anywhere. You can come and visit him tomorrow, if he makes it that far."

"What can we bring?" Mary Grace had produced a note-pad and was writing things down. "Toys? His bed?"

"How much is this going to cost?" Russ asked, louder than he'd meant. He felt the crossfire of shocked looks from Mary Grace and the vet. "I don't want to take on more than we can manage."

"Enough to remind you to get your dog's vaccines from now on," the vet said, scrawling on Francis's chart. "Now go home and start praying."

"We're ahead of you there," Russ muttered, grateful for Mary Grace's hand steering him back out to the waiting room. "We've got God's Marine at home."

The first thing Tracy did was collect Francis's things—his food and water bowls, a rubber chew toy Russ had bought, the washcloth he loved to tug on. She piled them by the door to bring to the clinic as soon as he was well enough to play. "Don't get your hopes too high, honey," Russ said, stroking her hair. He'd gone back to his dog book and reread: at ten weeks, a fifty-fifty chance.

Tracy shook her head with a heavy smile and fingered her rosary. "You told me the doctor said to pray." She slipped to her knees, crossed herself, and waited for Russ to kneel awkwardly beside her before she began. They were on the third decade, Tracy prompting Russ when he hesitated, before Mary Grace came in from the laundry room; she said, "The miracles seem to have started already," then set down the towels to join them. That night he heard Tracy and Mary Grace saying the rosary again, and again the next morning.

"You're going to wear that out," he said to Tracy, fingering the warm beads when she and her mother were done.

"Have you called the clinic yet?" she asked.

"He's hanging on." While Russ had had the receptionist on the phone he asked how much of a tab they'd run up so far; only two hundred dollars was left from his bonus. "One eighty-five," she said. "Without the lab work. We've got him on a drip and the heat lamp, which are extra." Her voice softened. "He's a pretty dog. I had a basset hound when I was a girl; I never loved a dog more." This kept Russ from telling her to unplug the heat lamp. Still, that night, when the message from the clinic hadn't changed, he brought it up again with Mary Grace. "If he doesn't get better soon—we can't afford much more of this."

"What else is there to do? Russ, the dog is ours now. We have to keep going."

"And just pay and pay?"

"I was thinking pray and pray," she said dryly.

"You're a regular Gracie Allen. Those prayers don't come free. We cleared the two-hundred-dollar mark this afternoon." Mary Grace looked startled, which gratified Russ. "And they aren't even saying he's stable yet. We may only be prolonging things."

"We can't just let him die."

"We can't force him to live." Although Russ would have, if he could have thought of a way. He found himself listening for the pup's heavy step, his deep bark, comical from such a young dog. Once while Mary Grace and Tracy were praying he put his face next to the puppy's blanket and tried to hold himself inside Francis's warm, clean smell.

Mary Grace stood up now and gestured for Russ to follow her. She led him to Tracy's room and leaned against the door, listening without a hint of embarrassment. Russ leaned in, too. "Please," Tracy was saying, and he could hear the tears crowding her voice, the desperation. "Please, please, please," the last one like a growl. And then she almost shouted. "Please!" It took Russ a moment to register that this wasn't the voice of supplication; it was the voice of demand.

"Please," murmured Mary Grace, looking at him.

"To please Tracy," he murmured back. The next morning, after he called the clinic to hear that the dog's lungs seemed to be clearing but his fever wouldn't break, and after he calculated that they could manage another day in the clinic if he put off the new suit he'd already put off for so long, he told Mary Grace that she should have God get on the stick. Tracy came down to breakfast with a face the color of sand.

"They think he might be getting better, honey," Russ said. She nodded. He went on, "His temperature's still up, but he's breathing better." When she still didn't respond, he prodded. "Isn't that good news?"

"Better? What's better? He's dying." She put down her spoon and tore away from the table; he could hear her sobs even after she slammed her bedroom door. At the same time Patrick shouted, "Mom? What did you do with my shirt?" Mary Grace got up without looking at Russ, and he finished his coffee, his hands moist with unease, before he went to console Tracy.

He'd expected her to be on her knees again, but she had flung herself across the bed, which rattled under the force of her weeping. "He's getting better, honey," he said softly, standing next to the bed. "He's pulling through."

"That's a lie," she shouted into her pillow.

"Francis is counting on you," Russ said, swallowing, imagining what Mary Grace would say. "He needs your prayers. You can't let him down now."

"Francis would be home already if God listened to my prayers," she said.

"Mine, too," Russ said, thinking of the metastasizing bill. "But God doesn't work that way. You have to keep asking."

"God doesn't work at all," she said, finally turning to look at him, her face rubbery and dull with tears. "And Francis is going to die."

"What will you think if he doesn't?"

Tracy curled her lip. "Big deal. So he was lucky this time. He could still get hit by a truck." Russ, speechless, stared at his daughter until she said, "Look, would you just go away? Can I have two minutes to myself?" The face she turned to him, wiped clear now of both tears and piety, could have been forty years old instead of ten. Russ groped down the hall to the bathroom, where he rested his face against the cool tiles. *Please,* he thought helplessly, his mind filled with Tracy's forbidding face. "Come back," he said aloud, knowing that anyone walking past would think he was praying for Francis.

"His fever's broken. He was able to drink some water." Mary Grace had Russ called out of a meeting to tell him.

"Thank God," he said. "What did Tracy say?"

"There's more."

"Can I bring him home today?"

"Russ," Mary Grace said, and he heard the edge to her voice. "When the fever broke they knew for sure. He's blind."

Russ's head snapped back; he clutched at the edge of the desk. "It happens sometimes, with distemper," Mary Grace was saying. "They weren't sure; they did everything they could. He's so young, they say he'll accommodate very well."

"For God's sake." Russ pressed his hand to his face. His book hadn't mentioned aftereffects; all he could think of now was Francis's prankster expressions, his merry-mournful face. It was more than he could stand.

"You can pick him up on your way home. They'll have the bill ready then."

"Have you told Tracy?"

"She went out as soon as I told her." Mary Grace paused, then went on without a hint of irony. "She left her rosary on the dining room table. Better start praying on this one yourself."

He did, if being unable to concentrate and muttering Tracy's and Francis's names all afternoon could be called prayer. He kept patting things: his checkbook, his own eyes. How could a dog be blind? Dogs *led* the blind. Russ had watched Francis watching Tracy; how would he watch for her now? Russ patted the pen on his desk and wished fiercely that he had never brought this puppy into their house.

Unshielded as he felt, it took all his strength to walk into the clinic for Francis. The puppy the receptionist brought to him was trembling, and so thin that Russ's throat clenched; the skin looked like a loose sack draped over bones. At the sound of Russ's voice Francis turned his droopy face up and twitched his tail.

"His care comes to six hundred and seventeen dollars," the receptionist said, stroking Francis's ear. "You're smart to take him home to recuperate. They always do better at home."

"I can only give you two hundred right now," Russ mumbled.

"We'll set up an account. Now, we'll need to see Francis back in ten days. Would you like to set up a vaccination schedule, too?"

Russ nodded, unable to speak. When he looked down the puppy was groggily sniffing Russ's tie. Light blue rings had settled over each pupil, and the pupils didn't move at all. After clearing his throat twice, Russ said, "Isn't there any chance he'll get his vision back?"

"You're lucky he made it." She wiggled Francis's ear, and he turned in the direction of her hand. "He's a tough guy. He'll be fine. You'll see."

But Russ, who cradled Francis's knobby, uncomplaining body back out to the car, didn't think he would see that. Before he even started the car, he put his face down to Francis's fur, which smelled like sour chemicals, and cried until the dog pulled himself up, turned laboriously around on the seat, and licked his fur dry.

Mary Grace was waiting for them at the door with Francis's blanket; when she held it up to him, he sniffed and whined, the first sound he'd made since they left the office. "Hey, skinny boy," Mary Grace cooed, stroking his belly. "We're going to have to feed you lots of fat now." Anyone would have thought she took in blind dogs every day. Francis lapped out his tongue in the direction of her voice.

"Where's Tracy?" Russ asked.

"In her room. She doesn't want any dinner. She doesn't want to be bothered."

"What are we going to do?"

"I talked about love and sacrifice and I promised ice cream. I'm out of ideas."

Russ sighed and slung the dog up higher on his shoulder, the position he'd used to carry five babies, and started down the hall. When Mary Grace said, "What are you going to say?" he shrugged. His best hope was that something wise would just come out of his mouth.

The words, when he opened her door, were "Hi, Tracy." She looked up from her book, her lips drawn thin and hard. "Look who wants his girl."

Carefully he squatted down and let Francis slip onto the floor. The dog sniffed in a tight circle, shaking his head over and over. Tracy put the book in front of her face. "What's he supposed to do now?" she said. At the sound of her voice Francis stood up and moved toward her, but he banged into the bed frame, which he barked at.

"Tracy," Russ pleaded. He lifted Francis and put him on the bed next to her, and she flinched away.

"He's not *allowed*."

"This is special."

"What, is it going to be special from now on?"

"Yes," said Russ.

The dog's feet slid on the slippery bedspread until he was lying down. He sighed and made a smacking noise, then curled up with his head resting on Tracy's knee.

She didn't make a sound, even when tears dripped from her face onto her T-shirt, and she didn't move.

"No matter what you think, he thinks he's your dog," Russ said.

"Well, he's wrong. You brought him home. He's yours."

"Now's when he needs you, Tracy. Now's when it counts."

"Look at him!" she shrieked, her voice so ragged that Francis shook his head again fiercely, his long ears flapping like heavy cloth. "He walks into things. What am I supposed to do, say 'Look out for that tree, Francis'?"

"He can accommodate. A dog has hearing, smell."

"He can't see me," Tracy snapped.

"He doesn't need to. He knew who he wanted to be next to." And then, very softly, "He was lucky."

Maybe Tracy didn't hear Russ. She said, "I can't carry him everywhere. It'll be too hard."

"Things are always harder than they seem," Russ said, skating now, saying things he'd certainly have to undo later. "You prayed for a puppy."

"Not like this. Besides, you prayed, too. And Mom."

"That's right," said Russ. "It's our fault, too." He rested his hand on the bedpost and closed his eyes, so he didn't see Tracy lift the puppy's head to look at it. "I'm so sorry, Trace," Russ whispered. He waited for her to reassure him, but she was looking at her dog, and had nothing to say.

RUSS
(1991)

Quietly, a month after her husband's funeral, Mary Grace bought a piano. An ad ran in the biweekly East Gables throwaway, which she now had time to read front to back: "Upright spinet-style. Much loved. Needs a new home." Mary Grace hadn't played since she was a girl, and the notion hooked into her imagination; piano playing seemed a gracious thing for a widow to do. Before she could lose her nerve, she called the number.

"I was about to give up on it," the woman told her. "I thought everybody would want a piano. Turns out nobody wants one."

"My husband always meant to get one. I don't know why we didn't."

"It's a hard thing," the woman said vaguely, so that Mary Grace didn't know whether she meant death or piano playing.

"I played when I was a girl. Now I'm old, and I'm going to learn how to play again," Mary Grace said, laughing a little at her own foolishness.

The woman laughed with her. "You have courage."

"Hardly," Mary Grace said. "Just time." Then she hung up and wrote Russ all about it.

She had started writing him letters while he was still in the hospital, not knowing what else to do with the words that rose up. *Indulge an old woman,* she wrote now on a lined tablet. *You never had to live in this house alone. You don't remember what silence sounds like.* And then, after thinking for a moment, *No one but you would think twice about a widow playing "How Great Thou Art."* Mary Grace smiled. Russ had hated "How Great Thou Art," the most unsingable song in the hymnal, and the comfort that came in that homey memory was almost enough to balance, for a moment, her grief.

He had gone quickly, his decline unwavering; the man had been headstrong even in death. Sick only two days before he saw the doctor, he lived three months more, long enough for all of the children to come and sit beside his bed before the cancer finally carried him away. Eighty-two years on the earth, Father Dennis kept saying in his eulogy—fine years, full years. Mary Grace had sat nodding idiotically while her daughter, Tracy, clutched her hand. Russ had tasted, the priest maundered on, all that life held out, and Mary Grace nodded like a waggle-headed doll even though this young man was dead wrong. She said so later, in the hot afternoon while her children sat dull and damp eyed. "Your father never had to go to his spouse's funeral," she said. Tracy frowned and started to close in until Mary Grace flapped her away. "I'm just telling you the truth. And another thing—your father never had to see me buried."

"Go get 'em, Mom." Paul, her oldest, still her pet, grinned.

"He never robbed a bank. He wasn't in the movies. For Pete's sake. Nobody has tasted all that life holds out. I wish they wouldn't let children conduct funerals."

"What should the priest have said?" Tracy sniffed.

"Life is tiny. *Tiny*. We don't get to do half of what we want," Mary Grace said.

"Dad told me no life could have treated him better," Kevin offered from the buffet.

"He lied," Mary Grace said. "He wanted a million dollars. Don't look so shocked; he didn't take some awful secret to the grave. He loved you all. But he still never got to meet Brigitte Bardot." Mary Grace sighed, seeing Tracy's eyes well up. "A joke," she said.

"This is no time to make a joke."

"Your father would have said it was the best time."

"Dad's jokes were always funny," Tracy snapped.

"You didn't think so when he called you Racy Tracy," Mary Grace snapped back, and watched her daughter shake her head furiously, like a dog.

"Why are you doing this? Can't you just once let us love him?"

"I want you to love him all the time," Mary Grace said. She was confused, half offended. "I just want you to love who he was. He wanted things! He was never satisfied a day in his life. Oh, this is basic. Didn't you ever see the man at all?" Her raised voice cracked at the edges, and all five of her children were frozen in front of her, their mouths ajar—Russ's very expression. Some complicated emotion climbed up Mary Grace's throat and she felt her mouth go shapeless. "A legacy," she managed to say. "Next time you want something, remember that your father wanted it, too. Every time you yearn, he's alive in the world."

"Jesus, Mom. Is this the best you can do?" Kevin said.

She knew better than to say *My loss is greater than yours. I want things you've never even thought about,* but the words flew away from her—just as well, she would think later. "I never knew another soul as well," she said.

So now they were all angry with her. James and Kevin couldn't bring themselves to answer her phone calls, and Paul's voice sounded distant when he called on Sunday afternoons, his conversation so jaunty it left her worn out. *I've got a gift for annoying them,* she wrote to Russ. *If you had said those things, you and the kids would have wound up drinking margaritas and playing Scrabble.* He would have won, too, nobody noticing until the end how he quietly spelled his way to the triple-score squares with dull words like *box* and *donkey.*

Mary Grace had the alphabet on her mind now that she had bought sixteen dollars' worth of sheet music and was trying to remember how to read it—first B, then G, counting up the lines and spaces. Frowning at the music and then looking down at her hands, ugly as crabs on the keyboard, she picked her way through. Her fingers collapsed or skated off the keys, and the ring fingers were too weak to make any sound at all. After five minutes she had to stop and shake her stinging hands, plunge them in warm water.

She knew perfectly well that she was playing balky, old-lady versions of "The Lord's Day" and "Light of Life." *I make this piano wheeze,* she wrote to Russ. But she kept at it. For five, sometimes ten minutes a day she was at peace, and had sense enough to be grateful.

One day the phone rang while she was working out some tricky fingering, and she let it go. Her spirit of gratitude moved her to stay right where she was through fifteen rings. Once she could play the phrase without stopping, she stood up and made herself a congratulatory cup of tea, feeling for the first time in months something like the old, fierce satisfaction. "Thank you," she murmured automatically, bobbing her head. It was as close as she'd come to prayer since the funeral. When Russ had been alive, she'd done the praying for both of them, constant muttered intercessions for his business, his health, his faith. Now she couldn't fix on anything to thank or ask for, and she got a little jolt of delight from eating dinner without first blessing the chop or chicken breast. During Mass on Sundays she made quiet lists in her pew—groceries, chores, hymns she meant to learn.

The phone rang again as she was washing lettuce, and then a half-hour later, while she ate. Mary Grace had never let a phone go unanswered in her life. Ha! She didn't have to do anything. Tomorrow she would buy roast beef for dinner—the expensive kind, already cooked.

Past eight, finally, when she was settled in front of the TV, the doorbell rang over and over, as if someone were punching out a code. "Hold your horses," Mary Grace said, easing up from her chair. The door was shaking slightly under the force of dull pounding by the time she got there and called out, "Who? Who's there?"

"Grandma?"

"My Lord in heaven," Mary Grace said, yanking at the dead bolt and chain locks. "Kate."

"Where have you been?" the child cried as she swung open the door. "No one answered the phone. I was cold."

Mary Grace pulled her in—stick-thin arms, tangled red hair, and eyes red, too, lips swollen and chewed. Her only granddaughter, Kevin's oldest child, not a child at all anymore, two years at a conservatory in Minnesota. "What are you doing here? Where's your father?"

"Why didn't you answer the phone?"

"I never imagined it might be you. Oh, child," Mary Grace said, pulling the girl into her arms, feeling the knobs of her spine underhand. "Don't you eat anymore?" she murmured into Kate's ear without letting her go.

"They don't give me what I want."

"Does your father know you're here?"

"Don't tell him," Kate said, nestling against Mary Grace's shoulder as if she meant to stay there.

"Not a chance," Mary Grace said.

Kate lifted her head and gave Mary Grace a watery smile. "I had to come," she said, and then, looking over her grandmother's shoulder, cried, "Why is there a piano here?"

"It's mine," Mary Grace said before she could stop herself, or stop Kate from going to it. "Of course, you can use it. I just want my little practice time every day."

Kate was already stooping over the keyboard, unwinding silky arpeggios. "Did you know? How could you know?" she mumbled. "In tune, too. Something knew. Things don't let go that easily."

"I needed a little companionship," Mary Grace said,

watching her granddaughter seat herself and push back the music rack. "Do you want tea?"

"Extra sugar," the girl called out and then started to play loud and crashing scales, which suited Mary Grace's mood nicely.

Later, after she showed Kate where the foldaway bed was and found her a pillow, Mary Grace was all for letting explanations wait until morning, but the girl insisted on telling everything at once, putting away cup after cup of oversweet tea. She had walked out on her scholarship. After twelve years, she couldn't play one more note of Bach or Handel; the music had fled. "I went to a Mozart festival and didn't hear any of it. I mean I really didn't hear it. Do you believe me?"

Mary Grace nodded, thinking of the times she sat calculating expenses while a homily washed over her. "I guess your father doesn't understand."

Kate nodded so hard that drops of tea flew onto the sheets. "We fight. He says I've got a God-given talent."

"Your father says that?"

"He doesn't know where else it could have come from." Kate leaned forward and clamped her wiry hands around Mary Grace's wrists. "I don't hear it. I used to hear music all the time, but now the notes all run together—I might as well be listening to a car crash. My teachers tell me to listen and I hear the five o'clock rush hour. What am I supposed to do with this?" The girl was at the brink of tears, her voice scraped and raw. "You know, don't you? I need for you to tell me."

Words rose up to Mary Grace's mouth as if she'd spent a lifetime counseling musicians. "You're doing exactly the right thing. This is just where you should be," she said, and held her bony granddaughter's hand when the girl sighed and curled back against the pillow, her mouth forming bodiless, grateful words as she plummeted into sleep.

Kate refused to call her father, even when Mary Grace chided her that he would be imagining a figure crumpled under a bridge or leaning against some ominous storefront. The girl hit a sour chord and held it with the pedal. "He says bad news always gets delivered. That's what he said the day he got the letter from my dean."

"You can't go into hiding. I'll call him myself."

"He'll tell you the same thing," she said.

Mary Grace called Paul first, as a warm-up. "He won't let her stay there, Mom," Paul said. "He probably shouldn't. The college will give her scholarship back; they just want her to do what she said she'd do."

"She doesn't believe in it."

"Belief and a buck will buy her a Coke," Paul said, Russ's old phrase. "I can't believe I have to explain this to you. Are you turning into a Good Cop in your twilight years?"

"The position has come open," Mary Grace said. She didn't hang up until he promised he would take her side with Kevin—even though Paul said she was getting in the middle, and no one ever thanked the middleman. "Kate's thanking me," Mary Grace said, peering around the corner to watch her granddaughter, hair brilliant in the sunlight, writing on a pad propped against the music stand.

Kevin called at exactly six that night, as soon as the rates went down. "Let me talk to my daughter," he said when Mary Grace answered. Kate slipped away from the table, making a throat-slitting gesture with her finger, and Mary Grace smiled at her and nodded.

"Hello to you, too, son."

"Very cute. I can't believe the things you'll do. We've been out of our minds."

"She's fine, just a little thin. Doesn't this child eat?"

"Let me talk to her." His voice was thick with frustration.

"She's not ready to talk," Mary Grace said pleasantly. "She's safe here. I have a piano."

"Good, Mom. Great. You just crack the whip over her. Make sure she's practicing for the Bach festival. There are people coming from Germany to hear her—did she tell you that? If they like her, they'll offer her a position."

"She'll be ready to surprise them," Mary Grace said, trying to cover her own surprise. "God-given talent. Where's your faith, son?"

A hard noise came through the receiver, loud enough to hurt, followed by a dial tone; he must have hurled the phone at the wall. The only one of the boys who had a temper. Russ had called him The Wrath of God when he was out of earshot.

Mary Grace moved to the living room, where Kate was noodling softly at the piano. "You might have told me," Mary Grace said.

"It doesn't make any difference. I can't play for them."

"They're coming from Germany."

"I told the dean to cancel the trip."

"Maybe the dean knows a little more than you do," Mary Grace said, and Kate rolled her eyes. "All right then, miss. Play for me. Show me what happens."

"I *told* you. I *can't*," Kate wailed.

"Show me. Then I can tell your father."

Kate stared at the keys for a long time before sitting up. She lifted her chin, raised her hands to shoulder height, and let them fall, the fingers already moving. The piano seemed to groan and struggle to keep up with the girl's reckless playing—hell-bent for leather, like a skier bombing straight downhill. She didn't hit a wrong note, though, and Mary Grace couldn't help admiring that, even though the girl played as though she was disgorging something. Finally, in the middle of a phrase, Kate stopped. "Happy now? That's what it sounds like." She spat, actually spat, on Mary Grace's carpet.

"Where do you think you are? Go clean that up," Mary Grace said, outraged, and when the girl returned with paper towels, Mary Grace said, "You have to go back."

"It's not music. I can't find the music anymore."

"It's close enough to pass," Mary Grace said.

Kate leaned against the wall and started to sob. Mary Grace left her alone; she believed the girl's torment, but hearing her play changed everything. What Kate had was like a sickness. She needed the help of people who knew how to treat music that snarled from the piano.

Finally Kate's weeping began to quiet. Without turning her face from the wall, she said, "I talk to them. Bach and Mozart. Liszt. Does that seem crazy?" Mary Grace shook her head. "I had their pictures up in my room when I was little. I'd pray to them like saints. Pray for an octave-and-a-half reach. Got it, too."

"Maybe they are saints," Mary Grace said.

"I prayed to get the scholarship. To play the third movement of the Italian. But I never thought I'd have to pray to understand the notes." She reached down to the keyboard and plunked out a crude scale with her forefinger. "It's all the same. It's all dead."

"You're young," Mary Grace said. "You'll turn a corner and hear beautiful things, music. Better than ever. You'll laugh at yourself."

"Everybody says this is serious. That's what I'm trying to tell you. What good is a scholarship? I'm high and dry." She rubbed her eyes—the tears wouldn't stop slipping out—and Mary Grace tried to make some joke about dryness, but she couldn't find it. "Music was the only thing I believed in," Kate said. "Now what am I supposed to do?"

"I think you're supposed to pray."

"To who? St. Mozart? St. Liszt? Liszt was no saint."

"He's a start," said Mary Grace.

The next morning Mary Grace put on slacks and edged into the narrow closet next to Kevin and Paul's old room. She spent ten minutes groping around coverless books and deflated volleyballs before she found the box she was looking for, LPs dating from the sixties.

Kate was hunched at the piano, poking at one key over and over. She didn't look up until Mary Grace lowered the record player needle onto Brahms's first piano concerto, the music fuzzy through the album's pops and scratches. Then Kate covered her ears.

"Are you trying to get rid of me?"

"We bought one a month," Mary Grace said. "After dinner we would come in here and listen."

"You must have gotten indigestion."

"It was your grandfather's idea. He believed in culture. He said you've got to have something to steer by."

"Nobody could steer by this," Kate said, shuddering in the direction of the record player.

"For someone with such sensitive hearing, you don't listen very well," Mary Grace remarked.

Kate tossed her head and started to play, deliberately out of sync with the record, loitering over a phrase and then tearing ahead, adding trills to the most discordant parts. Mary Grace went to the piano and dropped the lid over the keys; Kate moved her hands out of the way just in time. She backed up the piano bench in order to stand, but Mary Grace pushed her back down. "Pay attention!" she said.

Mary Grace was unexpectedly happy. Listening to the record she'd forgotten, she felt warmth moving through her—the music so sweet, almost bursting. Russ used to sit with damp eyes. Memory gave way to memory, and Mary Grace closed her own eyes and wondered why they never bought the vacation house they had talked about, the cat, the boat. A boat! Light and trim, quick—one year she and Russ had even gone downtown to the boat show, collected pamphlets. Why had so much gone undone? If she'd understood, she would have been better, gentler, more giving, but she'd never really believed he could be vacuumed cleanly out of her life. She let the tears slip out.

"Oh, Grandma," Kate said, and Mary Grace felt the uncertain tap of the girl's hand. "It isn't worth it. At least let me get you a better recording. This one was never very good."

"Try to have a little respect," Mary Grace said. "Listen and learn." Kate succeeded this time in standing up, banging into her grandmother and running up the stairs, weeping. Mary Grace closed her eyes again and didn't try to stop her. The girl would learn whether she listened or not.

Mary Grace went back to the closet later that day and pulled out the rest of the records. She stacked them up on the spindle five at a time, so that Kate, glancing in, said, "I guess you're trying to make a point." But she smiled. After lunch she even played an imitation of the Mendelssohn for Mary Grace, including the skip in the second movement, until Mary Grace muttered, "Very funny." She wanted to laugh, but her throat closed and she couldn't say any more; it was the sort of joke Russ would have relished.

After dinner that night, when the two of them were sitting in front of the TV shouting answers to game-show contestants, someone rang the doorbell, stabbing at it so that the bell chattered. "Uh-oh," Kate said. "The long arm." Sure enough, when Mary Grace opened the door, Kevin glared back at her and called to his daughter, "I brought a new coat for you."

"Come in," Mary Grace said.

"We're flying out tomorrow," Kevin kept shouting over Mary Grace's shoulder. "We've got a meeting with the dean."

"It won't work," said Kate. "I can't play."

"Couldn't you have found her a conservatory closer to home?" Mary Grace asked.

"Some of the best musicians in the world—" Kevin said, and then, to Kate, "You won't get this chance again. It's now or never."

"That's what I'm banking on," Kate said, finally getting out of her chair but staying the width of the room from her father.

"Want some tea?" Mary Grace asked Kevin.

"I'm trying to talk to my daughter," he growled.

"She likes tea. You should know that. Kate, play for your father while I put the water on." Mary Grace turned her back on the girl's furious stare. "She was practicing just this afternoon," she said to Kevin. "I couldn't get her to stop."

"Nothing unusual about that," he said. "Professionals practice six hours a day."

"Go on now," Mary Grace said, patting Kate on her flat rump and turning toward the kitchen. She set down the cups and kettle gently so she could hear Kate trudge through a Brahms intermezzo. Mary Grace knew the girl was trying to play like a robot, but to her old ears the music still sounded beautiful.

"What the hell is that?" Kevin asked when Kate finished the coda.

"An homage to your youth," she said. Mary Grace heard the piano bench creak, and then a moment's silence. "For God's sake," Kevin said softly. She glanced around the kitchen door to see him holding an album jacket, brushing it lightly with his fingers. He looked up when he heard his mother. "I can't believe you kept these."

"You can't imagine I would have thrown them away," Mary Grace said.

"Jesus, I had completely forgotten. Patrick claimed he had an earache every night."

"I thought that was you."

"I was lying under the coffee table. Dad would mist up on Brahms, and I couldn't stand to look. The second piano concerto still makes me cry," Kevin said. His face held a tender, distant expression until Kate asked, "What did Grandma make you love?" and he snapped back into focus.

"St. Clare is the patron saint of television," he said, grinning as he always did when he had his mother over a barrel. "St. Fiacre, if you're dying of syphilis."

"Good Lord," Mary Grace said, feeling her face get hot and silly. "I would have thought you'd forgotten that."

"Not on your life. This is hard-won knowledge. St. Hubert for healthy dogs, but St. Sithney for mad ones. No saints for cats, which never seemed fair."

"What are you talking about?" Kate asked.

"One summer your grandmother made us read *The Lives of the Saints*. She quizzed us over dinners. Made us write papers."

"You exaggerate," Mary Grace murmured, embarrassed but amused, too, a smile fluttering on her mouth.

"'Cosmas and Damian: Holy Hairdressers,'" Kevin said triumphantly. "I used it in religion class the next year and got an A."

Mary Grace couldn't keep her own laughter back. "See? Practical application."

"You told us we were reading to find out how to live. When Paul said he didn't want to be a saint, you told him he still had a comfortable margin. You said you wanted us to have some options."

"Did I really?" Mary Grace said, whooping now.

"Dad always said you had a hard grip on holiness," Kate said.

"I got it from Russ," Mary Grace gasped. "'If a goal is worth anything, it should be the hardest thing you've ever done.' Then he'd tell me that was why he married me."

Kevin and Kate were abruptly silent; she could feel them drawing back. "It was a joke," she added, trying to squelch her mirth, but she could feel the rowdy laughter still banging around inside her.

"Your grandfather," Kevin said to his daughter, "was a great man. He had high principles. After sixty years, he still called your grandmother his bride."

"He had a fine sense of humor," Mary Grace said.

"He always looked on the light side."

"That man?" she cried. "He woke every day of his life ready to shoot himself. He laughed to keep himself from doing it."

"Oh Christ, this is you all over. He was a saint. A hero," Kevin said. "That just kills you, doesn't it?"

"Listen to me," she said, the lunatic laughter bubbling in her throat. "He was a hero, all right. Day after day, all he believed in was his own two feet. What do you think a hero is?"

"Schumann," Kate said. "He was one of the greatest performers in Germany. He hated the weakness of his fourth fingers, so he practiced for hours holding the fourth fingers out straight over the keys while his other fingers played. His arms would shake from exhaustion. Eventually his hands were paralyzed." She added, "I don't want to play that much."

After a pause, Kevin said to his daughter, "You can't turn your back on a talent like yours."

"Why not?"

"There's nothing else you know how to do," he said, not ungently.

Kate clenched her fists, but her fierce expression crumpled. Mary Grace closed her eyes. There was no point; she could never make either of them know what she knew. The laughter that had filled her was dribbling away, leaving her hollowed out. She scarcely bothered to hear Kate mutter, already defeated, "I can flip burgers. I can learn anything." The words pained Mary Grace—the girl didn't even believe herself. Before she had to listen to any more Mary Grace stiffly pulled herself up and announced that she was going to bed.

"We're leaving in the morning," Kevin said.

"Turn out the lights before you go upstairs," she said.

She woke deep into the night; the only sound was the furnace's thrum. The few times Mary Grace had lain wakeful when Russ was alive, she'd reached for her rosary, working through the decades for Russ and each of the children. Now prayers felt dim and hollow, so after shrugging uncomfortably against the pillow, she reached for her notepad, visible in the gray moonlight. Some of the phrases she recalled, but then there was a whole passage she barely remembered writing. Mary Grace squinted; it was her own straight hand. She tapped the pad, angry to see words she had so little memory of.

Do you still want a clematis by the mailbox? How can I keep from calling it Russ's memorial vine?

When Kate leaves, she'll want the piano. Nobody leaves without taking something. I meant to hang on, but she's already got good-bye all over her.

If I plant the clematis, what color? They have different shaped leaves. All these choices, but there are no right choices.

Still reading, Mary Grace groped on the bedside table for a pen and added in the margin, *There is nothing in heaven or on earth that I don't want,* the letters unnaturally heavy because of her awkward posture. Then she slowly sat up and swung her legs, one at a time, onto the floor, taking her time about standing up; her balance had been unreliable lately. She pulled on her robe and shuffled downstairs to the living room, where Kate was sleeping on the sofa, meaning only to look at the child while she still could. But Kate's eyes snapped open as soon as Mary Grace reached the doorway, and the two looked at each other in the dull light.

"Did I let you down?" Mary Grace asked, and Kate nodded. "Par for the course," Mary Grace said.

"I thought I'd be safe here."

"No one's safe," Mary Grace said. "Anywhere."

To Mary Grace's relief Kate grinned at her. "Grandmothers in books don't say things like that."

"I could use a book. Your grandfather said I always missed my cues."

"Do you miss him?"

"Oh, child," Mary Grace said, blinking. "It's like having no lungs."

Kate nodded. "Is that why you got the piano? At first I thought you got it for me."

"I needed to hear something. I was happy to hear you."

"I don't hear anything worth listening to. I used to hear music without even thinking about it. Now it's like there's no ground under my feet. Do you know what I mean?"

"I know exactly what you mean," Mary Grace said, bending down to stroke the blanket over the girl's foot. "Do you want the piano?"

Kate nodded without surprise. "You don't know what to do with it, do you?"

"I could bring it to you in Germany. Things will sound different there."

"German," Kate said, so deadpan it was a second before Mary Grace recognized the joke.

"You could show me Schumann's house," Mary Grace said.

"Maybe he's the one I should be praying to." Kate yawned, sliding down into the covers.

"He knew what he believed in. That's important," Mary Grace said. "But he was crazy."

Mary Grace straightened the edge of Kate's blanket and felt her way back up the stairs, trying with all her logic and memory to stop believing that Russ was waiting for her.